The Last Flight
of José Luis Balboa

The Last Flight of José Luis Balboa

STORIES BY *Gonzalo Barr*

A Mariner Original

HOUGHTON MIFFLIN COMPANY · BOSTON NEW YORK 2006

For information about permission to reproduce selections from
this book, write to Permissions, Houghton Mifflin Company,
215 Park Avenue South, New York, New York 10003.

Visit our Web site: www.houghtonmifflinbooks.com.

Library of Congress Cataloging-in-Publication Data
Barr, Gonzalo.
The last flight of José Luis Balboa : stories / Gonzalo Barr.
p. cm.
"A Mariner Original"
ISBN-13: 978-0-618-65886-2
ISBN-10: 0-618-65886-6
1. Miami—Fiction. I. Title.
PS3602.A77743L37 2006
813'.6—dc22   2006009765

Book design by Lisa Diercks
The text of this book is set in Filosofia.

Printed in the United States of America

MP 10 9 8 7 6 5 4 3 2 1

The following stories have been previously published in slightly
different form: "Braulio Wants His Car Back" in *Gulf Stream*,
volume 20; "The Sleepless Nights of Humberto Castaño" in *The
Street Miami*, June 2004; "Coup d'État" in *Gulf Stream*, volume 24.

Visit the author's Web site: www.gonzalobarr.com.

For Leejay Kline

Contents

Foreword

Not long ago, I heard a true story about a professor who was asked to judge a literary competition for a local community college. One Sunday morning, he sat down on his living room couch and began to look through the entries that were, he soon realized, unpromising. He divided the manuscripts into piles: awful, worse, and worst. And then he gave up and fled to the local bookstore to buy a copy of the Sunday paper.

While he was at the bookstore, a violent storm came up. Wind and rain made it impossible for him and his fellow customers to leave the store. When at last it subsided, he returned home to find that the storm had felled a tree that went through his roof and landed on the coffee table, the manuscripts — and the couch on which he had been sitting.

Judging this year's Bakeless Prize competition, I found myself thinking that, had I been that professor, and had *The Last Flight of José Luis Balboa* been among the entries in that competition, I would never have survived. For I would not have been able to bring myself to leave, to put down this engaging, funny, highly enjoyable collection of stories and take off in search of a lesser entertainment.

Gonzalo Barr's collection may remind you of why you would rather actually read than go to the bookstore. With their deceptively modest authority and just as deceptively easy charm, these narratives draw you in and make you want to find out what will happen next. What ill fortune will ensue when the Miami TV journalist in "Faith" overplays a story about a local religious sighting? Will the narrator of "Braulio Wants His Car Back" manage to reclaim his wife's Plymouth, which he lent to the friend who came over with him from Cuba on a raft made from inner tubes? What fate awaits the neighbors involved in the tragicomic love triangle at the center of "Coup d'État," a romantic imbroglio with surprising connections to the government of Venezuela? What even these scraps of plot make clear is that the tales in this collection concern not only individuals but a city, the vibrant, bilingual, and truly multicultural border city that is Miami, where so many residents haven't forgotten that they come from somewhere else and, like it or not, must straddle the two worlds of the old home and the new. Without strain or agenda, Barr's stories capture perfectly the moments of discovery and the areas of friction that inevitably occur when one country, one culture, or one language rubs up against another. The stories are rooted in individual lives and at the same time in the politics and immigration history of the last thirty years.

But finally, what's so memorable about *The Last Flight of José Luis Balboa* is not just its feeling for plot and background, for the subtle permeations of politics and culture, but the humanity with which Gonzalo Barr draws his varied characters, his sympathy for their aspirations and fears, for their insights and delusions, and for the way that their pasts inevitably come back to bite them in the present. These characters—their haplessness, their intelligence, their imagination, the courage and style and humor they show in the face of the unbeatable odds—are ultimately the reasons why this year's winner of the Bakeless Prize kept this reader on the couch.

Francine Prose
Judge, 2005 Bakeless Prize for Fiction

. . . Miami seemed not a city at all but a tale, a romance of the tropics, a kind of waking dream in which any possibility could and would be accommodated.

—Joan Didion, *Miami*

The Last Flight
of José Luis Balboa

Braulio Wants His Car Back

When Pepe Luis asks me if I know someone who is selling a car cheap, an old *cacharro* he can drive to work, I tell him, "*¡No jodas!*, just take my wife's Plymouth until she can drive again." My wife is recovering from a sprained back she got at work. She does not have to spend so much time at home, but the lawyer told us we would get more money that way.

Pepe Luis and I are *compadres*. Twenty-two years ago, he stole six inner tubes from the truck repair shop where he worked outside Havana. We roped together the inner tubes and in the middle of the night pushed off the beach to paddle north until we were caught by the Gulf Stream. For five and a half days we drifted across the Straits of Florida. We made landfall in the Keys. The following year was the Mariel boatlift, so we could have come over in a real boat, but who would have guessed something like that was going to happen. That was also the year I met my wife in Miami and got married. Eleven months later, she gave birth to our son. I asked Pepe Luis to be the godfather. When you share a six-by-eight-foot raft for over five days with a man who helps you survive thirst and hunger and the fact that everywhere you turn there is only water and sky, you become closer than brothers. Maybe my wife does not understand, but I am telling you that is the way it is.

So I lend Pepe Luis the car. I tell him that I will need it back as soon as my wife can return to work.

He says, *Sí, sí, sí* and *¿Cómo no?* and even *No problems*, an expression he says a lot now that he has decided to sound more American.

My wife yells at me for lending her car. I tell her that I lent it to Pepe Luis, but she does not care if I lent it to the Pope himself. She says that Pepe Luis is a thief who thinks that he is still in Cuba, where if you want anything you have to steal it. Then the lawyer calls and tells my wife that she can go back to work, and my wife says, "You see? Now I need the car." So I call Pepe Luis.

His wife answers the phone. Clara says that he is not there. I ask her to tell him that I will come by later in the week to pick up the car.

"What car?" she says.

"What do you mean 'what car'? How many cars do you have?"

"*Bueno*, I mean to say that Pepe Luis paid you for that car, no?"

"No, Pepe Luis did not pay me for that car. I lent it to him. It belongs to my wife, and I told him that she would need it back when she returned to work, which she is ready to do next week."

"I am very confused," Clara says.

I am not sure she understands me, or maybe she is making herself out to be the *chiva loca*, pretending not to know about the car.

"Please ask him to call me," I tell her. I am shaking my head when I hang up.

I wait through the rest of Tuesday and all of Wednesday, thinking that Pepe Luis is probably busy trying to find some form of substitute transportation. If you do not have a car, *mi hermano*, you are fried in this city because you cannot rely on the buses. Without a car, Pepe Luis could not work at the big construction projects all over town. So I understand. And I am willing to be patient.

On Thursday, I call him again. No one answers. *Leave a message at the beep*, he says on the answering machine, first in Spanish, then in his blenderized English.

"Pepe Luis? Braulio," I say. "I am calling because I need the car back. Remember, I told you . . ." And I go into the whole story that I already told you and that I told Pepe Luis too, when I first lent him the car, but that for some reason, he is now pretending to have forgotten. My doctor tells me that my blood pressure is high and that I should avoid getting excited, but this business with Pepe Luis is starting to *encojonarme*.

I am a patient man. I run a paint and dry wall business. I hire day laborers when I have the work. Some of the men are dumber than a mashed plantain, so I am constantly wrestling with my temper. At home, I want to relax. After dinner, I help my wife with the dishes. Then I watch TV in the family room.

Thursday becomes Friday and Pepe Luis does not call. My wife says he is avoiding me. My son, Rafaelito, who is studying to be a policeman, tells me that we should go to Pepe Luis's house and demand the car back. He wants to wear his uniform, which is an apprentice uniform, not even a proper policeman uniform, but he thinks it will impress Pepe Luis.

So we drive to Pepe Luis's house. My wife's car is parked in the yard in front of the laundry Pepe Luis and I built last summer, next to the metal toolshed. He and I laid the concrete floor, and I myself built the two columns that hold up the roof that extends from the side of the house and hangs over the washer and dryer. And I am thinking, *Chico*, this has to be a misunderstanding. Pepe Luis will surely answer the door, or maybe his wife will answer it, and we will get the car back.

A chainlink fence surrounds the house and the yard. A wide gate opens to the driveway, where the car is parked, and a more narrow gate leads to a cement path that ends at the front door. The narrow gate is closed but not padlocked.

Rafaelito goes ahead of me and opens the gate. It squeaks like it needs oil. Dogs start barking. We stop and listen, but it sounds like the dogs are tied behind the house, so we walk to the front door. I can see lights inside. Someone is watching television. My son rings the doorbell. And as we wait, I am thinking that he looks like a proper authority in his uniform, even if it is an apprentice uniform. I will be very proud of him when he graduates as a policeman. And as I am thinking this, the television set goes silent and all the lights, one by one, go dark. No one comes to the door. I want to be patient, but I am finding it harder and harder not to become *encojonado*.

"Pepe Luis, it is me, Braulio!" I yell at the door.

My son says, "Let me do this, Pipo." He knocks like he is about to punch his fist through the door, and yells, "Open the door now! We've got you surrounded!"

I stop him, and say "*¡Oye, oye!* What do you think you are doing?"

We cup our faces against a window and try to peer inside the dark house. And while we are doing this, my wife's car shoots out of the driveway and down the street. By the time we turn around and run after it, it is at the stop sign. The rear lights glow red for an instant, the tires squeal, and the car disappears around the corner.

We jump in my son's car and try to follow it, but it is useless. And as we drive home, I am thinking, So this is the way you want it, *cabrón*. OK. No more Mr. Nice Guy.

Rafaelito and I agree to wait until 2:00 in the morning. He tells me that is the best time to catch a fugitive. I find the spare key to my wife's car and put it in my pocket. I try to nap, but I am too nervous, even after my wife makes me drink some herbal tea that she says is supposed to calm me.

At 2:00, Rafaelito drives me back to Pepe Luis's house. He parks his car down the street, and we walk the rest of the way. All the lights in the house are off. My wife's car is back in the yard. Rafaelito opens the gate, and it squeaks again. I hear the dogs bark, but I know that they are tied behind the house. Using the spare key, I plan to get into my wife's car and drive off quietly. I hate to do it this way, but Pepe Luis leaves me no choice.

Then two German shepherds come out from behind the house and Rafaelito and I run back to the sidewalk, close the gate, and keep running. The dogs are at the fence, barking loudly. The house lights go on.

We drive for half an hour. Rafaelito wants to return and try again, but I remind him that Pepe Luis wakes up very early and will probably not go back to sleep, not after this.

Saturday I have to reschedule a job because of this problem with the car. On top of that, I have to leave the house because I cannot stand my wife nagging me about how stupid I was to lend Pepe Luis the car in the first place. The last thing she tells me is that she is going to buy a Cadillac from Puchito Motors on Eighth Street—you know, the place with the big sign that says NO CREDIT? NO PROBLEMS!—and that I am going to have to pay for it if I do not get her car back before Monday. Even with the money from the workers' compensation, we are in no position to buy a Cadillac from Puchito or anywhere else.

Rafaelito and I agree to meet that evening to plan something else. We are running out of time.

I go home and wait for my son. My wife is giving me the long face, not talking to me. Around 7:00, Rafaelito comes in with a paper bag from the grocery.

"Pipo, I have the perfect plan," he says.

"For your sakes, it had better work," my wife yells from the bedroom, where she is watching one of her *telenovelas*. My son and I say nothing. Then he unwraps two huge steaks.

"I am not hungry," I tell him.

"This is not for us, it is for Pepe Luis's dogs."

"*¡No jodas!* You are going to feed steak to the dogs?"

"Yes, but wait until you see the seasoning."

I slip on my glasses and take the small box that he hands me and hold the box in the light, so I can read the label.

"There is enough there to knock out a horse for a week. Two horses," he says.

"I do not want to kill the dogs," I tell him.

And I watch my son coat both steaks with the drug that will make the dogs go to sleep, so we can open the gate and get my wife's car back, so my wife can stop nagging me and I can maybe rest tomorrow, Sunday, before it is time to go back to work on Monday.

A little after 1:00 in the morning we park Rafaelito's car near Pepe Luis's house. My son unwraps the steaks and carries them. The smell from the steaks must be very strong because the dogs run out to the front yard almost as soon as we get there. But before the dogs bark my son throws the steaks over the fence. He has a good arm and the steaks land near the dogs. The dogs sniff the meat. Each one runs off with a steak to lie at opposite ends of the front yard. They hold the meat under their front paws and tear at it with their teeth. Neither dog looks our way. Rafaelito notes the time on his watch and we walk back to his car.

My son and I sit in the dark, waiting for the drug to work on the dogs. Then he says, "OK," and we get out and walk back to Pepe Luis's house. At first I cannot see the dogs. When we get closer, I see that they are on the ground. Even when we reach the gate, they do not move.

"He locked the gate," Rafaelito says.

"What?"

"He locked the gate. Look, he closed the fence behind the car. He probably locked that too."

"I cannot go back without the car," I tell him.

"Just a few more minutes, Pipo." He runs back to his car and returns with a pair of bolt cutters.

"I borrowed these from the police academy," he says. "I thought we would need them. When I open the fence, you can drive Mima's car out."

I feel proud of my son as I watch him cut through the padlock and open the fence. "OK," I tell him before he runs back to his car. I unlock the door of my wife's car as quietly as I can when an alarm goes off and the headlights start to flash on and off.

"*¡Cooooñoooo!*" I yell, but I cannot hear myself because the alarm is loud enough to wake the dead. I get in and slam the door and put the car in reverse when Pepe Luis comes running out of his house in his pajamas. I press the accelerator, but something is not letting the car move, and a lot of dust falls into the glare of the flashing headlights.

Pepe Luis lunges at my door. I lock it just in time, as he slaps at it. Then he runs behind the car and stands there, waving his hands in the air, yelling something that I cannot hear because of the alarm. I check the parking brake, put the car in reverse, and press the accelerator. The car lunges back. Pepe Luis leaps out of the way. And as I am pulling out of the driveway, I see the front bumper of my wife's car on the ground, a long thick chain wrapped around the bumper and around one of the columns that held up the roof over the laundry. The column is broken, the roof has collapsed over the washer and dryer, and dust is everywhere.

The rear bumper hits the street. I turn the steering wheel so much that I almost back up onto the curb. I put the car in drive and am about to accelerate again when Pepe Luis jumps on the hood. He is yelling. The alarm is blaring. And I am truly *encojonado* now because I know that replacing the bumper is going to cost me an eye.

I press the accelerator and go as fast as I can with Pepe Luis on the hood. The alarm has not stopped and the headlights are still flashing. I zigzag down the street to shake Pepe Luis off, but he hangs on, clenching his mouth. The crucifix at the end of the plastic rosary that my wife wrapped around the rearview mirror swings wildly.

I turn onto a street that ends in a canal and accelerate. I am going to get rid of this *cabrón*, once and for all. Before I get to the end, I brake hard. Pepe Luis goes flying into the water, and I turn the steering wheel as far as it will go, but it is too late. The lights of the house at the end of the street fly across the windshield. I hear the tires screech and a thump. Then the car tilts to the side and slides roughly down the embankment into the canal.

The car floats long enough for me to roll down the window and climb out. I am trying to swim, when I hear water gushing in through the open window and fill the inside of the car. The water laps over the hood and against the windshield. Soon, all I can see of the car are the trunk and the rear lights, still blinking, before they too go underwater. The alarm sounds muted as the car sinks deeper into the dark canal.

I am trying to swim with my work shoes on, the ones with the steel toes, but I can barely stay afloat. Then I hear someone panting. It is Pepe Luis. And I get all *encojonado* again and start to call him every name I can think of, starting with the letter A. I see that Pepe Luis is shouting at me too, but I cannot hear him because I am working my way down the alphabet, through one insult after another. I am at the letter G when I think that here we are, Pepe Luis and me, two middle-aged men, once again treading water, trying to stay afloat, in the middle of the night.

I pull myself out of the canal and stand, feeling like I weigh a million pounds because of the wet clothes, when my son drives up and, after him, a couple of police cars. They take us all to the station, even my son.

Inside the station everything is cold. Nobody says anything to us, except to wait here. My clothes are still wet, and I start to shiver. Then a police officer takes us to a room where a sergeant is writing at a metal desk.

Although the sergeant does not ask us anything, Pepe Luis starts to talk. The police officer brings a finger to his lips and shushes him, but Pepe Luis keeps talking. The sergeant prints neatly on the form and does not look up. I have to hand it to Pepe Luis, he can talk his way out of anything. But then he always goes too far.

He says that his wife is a Santería priestess, a very powerful one, but that she was never good at aiming her spells. This is the first time I hear that his wife is a Santería anything. The sergeant stops writing and looks at Pepe Luis, who has his head down, like he is examining the linoleum floor for gaps.

So last night, Pepe Luis says, his wife was casting a spell, something she does only while he is asleep because she knows that he does not like it when she does Santería. He is a devout Catholic, he says with such a *cara dura* that I manage not to roll my eyes. The spell was meant to go to Cuba, he says. You know, to Fidel, but with his wife having such bad aim a little of the spell must have splashed on him while he was sleeping in the bedroom because one minute he was dreaming and the next he was sitting up in bed, then standing, a red-hot itching all over his body. And here Pepe Luis stands on one leg, then the other, pretending to scratch his chest and thighs, to show the sergeant and the police officer how hot the spell was that his Santería wife cast. He was not thinking, he says, about anything except cooling off when he ran out of the house and drove into the canal. *"¡Qué va!"* Pepe Luis says, looking at the officer now, the spell was so hot that when he fell into the water steam rose all around him. He was lucky that his good friend Braulio showed up to help him. And here Pepe Luis slings a bony arm around me.

I turn to Rafaelito and hope he says something, anything, because I see myself spending the night leaning against the wall of a jail cell, while Pepe Luis sleeps soundly on the floor. My son gets the message and starts to talk, but the sergeant asks him to step into another room for a moment. And while we wait, Pepe Luis does not say anything, and neither do I, which is fine with me because it is only a few moments before Rafaelito comes back and says, "OK, Pipo, we can go."

The sky is beginning to lighten when my son drives us home. Pepe Luis sits in the back and stays quiet until we get to his house. He looks as if he is about to say something, but he must think better of it and steps out.

My son turns the car around while I watch Pepe Luis open the gate and walk to his house. All the lights are on again. The dogs are barking, but it sounds like they are tied up in the back. His wife comes out wearing a nightgown. She goes toward him, her arms open. He waves her off and walks to the driveway where the car had been.

"Wait," I tell Rafaelito.

We watch Pepe Luis drag the heavy chain and the bumper and toss them in the toolshed. His wife calls him to come inside, but he ignores her. Pepe Luis takes off the shirt of his pajamas and walks to the collapsed roof over the laundry. His back is knotty. He is still as skinny as when we got here from Cuba on the raft.

Using both hands, he lifts the roof a few inches before his arms start to shake. Now his wife is yelling at him, "No, mi amor. ¡No!"

I get out of the car and run to Pepe Luis and put one hand between his and the other to the right.

"OK," I say. And together we lift the collapsed roof and hold it up. Rafaelito stands on the other side of Pepe Luis. He is about to grab the edge of the roof, but I tell him to find something we can use to prop it up. I tell him to look in the toolshed, pointing to it with my chin. In the shed are blocks, sacks of concrete, two-by-fours, tools and belts, and even hard hats.

Pepe Luis starts to lose his grip, so Rafaelito grabs what is closest to him—a few concrete blocks to get some height and, upright on the blocks, the bumper of my wife's car.

At first the roof is not very stable resting on the end of the bumper, but after a few adjustments, we set it down and let go. I stand back and wipe my hands on my tee shirt.

The roof looks funny propped up on the bumper and the concrete blocks, like modern art.

"Braulio, I was going to return the car," Pepe Luis says. "That is the truth."

"I left messages with your wife for you to call me, and you never did."

"Clara is terrible about giving me any messages."

"I left messages on your answering machine."

"You did? I have told the children not to play with that machine."

"Rafaelito and I came by—"

"Really, Braulio—"

"And what about the car alarm and the chain?"

"A lot of cars are stolen around here. When I heard the alarm, I did not know it was you."

"You are making all this up, Pepe Luis."

"I swear on my children's heads," he says, kissing the tips of his fingers. "May lighting strike me down this instant if I am not telling you the truth."

"And what about that?" I say, pointing at the shed. "Do you plan to return the hard hats and the tools? What about those sacks of concrete?"

Pepe Luis is quiet. I am thinking that replacing the car will cost me a lot less than admitting to my wife that she was right about him.

Now his eyes are teary. He is very emotional. He gets excited about all sorts of things, like when a neighbor complained about his keeping a rooster in the backyard. Pepe Luis could not understand that most people do not want to be awakened at 3:00 in the morning by the crowing of an old rooster. He wipes his face with his hands. I want to show him that I am not mad, that I am willing to forgive him, so I pat his back. I can feel the bones just below his papery skin. I tell him not to worry.

"After everything we have been through," I say, "what is a car? Even if it means my having to put up with my wife and her long face for another week or two." And I force a chuckle, just to show Pepe Luis that I mean it. He nods and turns. And he hugs me.

Now I wish he were not so emotional.

"Come on," I tell Pepe Luis, and I try to break the hug, but he will not let go. I am thinking that Pepe Luis will have to release me eventually. Then Rafaelito and I will be able to go home and get some sleep. I am thinking this when Clara and the children come and spread their arms around us. I look at Rafaelito for help, but he is looking away. There is nothing I can do. So I pat Pepe Luis's back and keep my eyes fixed on the ground.

And while everyone is hugging and crying, I remember that I know a man who is selling a car cheap. Not an old *cacharro*. A Honda, I think. I promise myself to call the man tomorrow, maybe even today. It is Sunday, I know, but I am sure he will not mind my calling him on his day off, especially after I tell him what happened to my wife's car.

Coup d'État

1.

When the elevator doors opened, I saw my neighbor sitting next to the front door of the condo that he shared with his wife. They were in their late twenties and did not have any children. Their apartment faced the elevators, so you knew it when they fried fish or had an argument. Their arguments went something like: Yes you did, No I didn't, Yes you did, No I didn't.

My neighbor wore a pair of expensive running shoes, shiny black gym shorts, a gray sweatshirt, and a baseball cap backwards. Every piece of clothing had the same logo and looked pristine. He sat with his knees close to his face.

I walked toward my own condo and turned the corner when I heard his wife's voice. "I've never met anyone so egotistical."

I peeked around the corner. His wife held a key with both hands and jammed it into the lock.

"This is the third time this week that you forgot your keys," she said. "I can't believe how selfish you are. You think that you are the center of the universe."

My neighbor raised his arms, elbows out, and plugged each ear with an index finger.

The next time I saw my neighbor, we met in the lobby and rode the elevator to our floor. I had just finished my morning walk. He was holding his mail.

"Did you hear about the protests?" he said. "Everybody is protesting against Chávez. This is it. We are going to get rid of him."

"But you just elected him."

"*I* didn't. Workers. The lower classes," he said, wrinkling his nose. "Chávez is another Castro."

I hardly knew my neighbor. Earlier that year, I had spoken to his wife after I discovered that she was the one who monopolized the only washing machine on the floor. She put their clothes in the washer and, once the tub filled with water, she unplugged the machine before disappearing for the rest of the day. When I figured out who it was, I knocked on their door.

She was polite and had the good looks of someone who could have been a cover girl once. I told her about the clothes. She looked at me as if she didn't know what I was talking about. Then she slapped her forehead and apologized. But it didn't stop. After a few more times, I pulled their wet clothes out and put mine in.

On our way up in the elevator, my neighbor introduced himself. He spoke very fast. His name was Benny, he said. He came from an old political family who had governed Venezuela for years before Chávez. He spent a semester at the London School of Economics. His classmates there called him Venny Benny on account of his nationality. A Sikh came up with the name, he said, moving his hands above his head as if he were wrapping cloth around it. His wife's name was Iris. She was a finalist for Miss Venezuela 1992, Benny said.

That last part I could believe. We reached our floor. He took a deep breath.

After London, he went home to work for his family, but he wanted to start his own business, so he came to Miami. He sold real estate over the Internet. Exotic, pricey locales, he said. He gave me his card. Ven/Ben was the name of his company.

"How is it going?" I asked him.

"How can it be going with Chávez scaring off investors?"

"Why not go back and do something about it?" I joked.

Just then a woman wearing too much makeup appeared around the corner and called the elevator. She was the wife of a retired county judge who for years presided over a successful TV show called *Gotcha!* The aim of the show was to catch adulterous spouses in the act and get them to reform. Reruns still aired late at night. The judge and his wife lived down the hall from Benny. We both said hello. She smiled and nodded. Benny changed the subject and talked about his plans to take up jogging, all the while patting his stomach, sucking it in.

The judge's wife stepped into the elevator and the doors closed.

Benny leaned close to me, and in a low voice said, "Why don't I do something about it? Oh, but I will." He narrowed his eyes, tapped his temple, and nodded.

For three months I did my laundry without incident. Until one Saturday afternoon, Iris caught me removing their clothes from the washer.

"Did I forget again?" she said.

Iris was barefoot. She wore a tee shirt that reached halfway down her thighs. The tee shirt lay tight and smooth against her body, showing none of the marks that suggested she wore anything underneath.

I stepped aside while she pulled their clothes out of the washer and tossed them in the dryer. She had long fingers and her tee shirt smelled faintly of lavender. She wore a ring with the biggest diamond I had ever seen. I asked her about Benny. She said that he was out working on a project.

"For his business?" I asked.

"No." She kept putting their clothes in the dryer. The dryer drum amplified her voice. "He wants to overthrow Chávez. He is out talking to every Venezuelan he knows in Miami, organizing a protest at the consulate."

The Venezuelan consulate was a block away from where we lived, a ten-story glass and steel building with a brutal-looking fountain in front of it made of brass rods that formed a fist of water in a bowl of gray concrete.

"He is convinced," Iris said, "that he can overthrow the president of the republic." She put the last of their clothes in the dryer.

I put my own clothes in the washer. When I finished, Iris was looking at me.

"Come," she said. I followed her down the hall into their apartment.

Hanging on every wall of the living room were pictures of Iris. A large gilt-framed photograph of her standing on stage with the other pageant finalists dominated the wall behind the sofa. Iris stood in the center of the living room, turning as if she were looking at the pictures for the first time. She turned until her eyes met mine.

"Sit down," she said. "I'll get you something to drink." Then she went into the kitchen.

She returned with two glasses of white wine and gave me one. The other she put on the coffee table in front of her. She sat in an overstuffed chair, carefully pulling down the end of the tee shirt with both hands. I sat on the sofa and put my glass next to a large leatherbound photo album that was the centerpiece of the table.

"Benny is out a lot and I get bored," Iris said, after taking a drink. "It's nice to have someone to talk to. Even when Benny's here, we don't talk. He says I talk too much. Every night we have quiet time."

"Quiet time?"

"Benny says he can't think if I'm talking all the time, so starting last month, every night from eight to ten, we don't talk to each other. No TV or music either. He thinks for two hours every night."

She looked at my glass. I picked it up but didn't drink.

Iris told me that she met Benny in Caracas, at an exclusive gym where every girl who wants to be a beauty queen goes to train. "It's also a place where you can meet a good catch," she said.

"Like Benny?" I said.

She said she recognized Benny's last name; the rest she learned later. "You married?" she asked me.

I shook my head.

"But you have lady friends, no? You're not gay, are you?"

"No," I said.

"There's nothing wrong with it," she said. "I think my husband is gay. He goes weeks, and *nada*," she said, motioning with her free hand as if she were wiping a slate clean.

I put my glass down.

"You know, he's manic-depressive." She took another drink. "He was being treated at home, but after a few public incidents, his father wanted him out of the way."

"I'm sorry."

"I manage. Anyway, his father helps us. He was a senator when I met Benny. Everybody thought he would be the next president. The way I figured it, if I wasn't going to be Miss Venezuela at least I'd be the president's daughter-in-law. So much for my plans." She raised her glass as if making a toast and drank it. "His father bought this condo for us. Not bad, no?"

I looked around as I was expected to do. The furniture was trendy, probably expensive, possibly Italian. I ran my hand flat against a seat cushion.

"On his good days," she said, "Benny can be sweet and considerate. On his manic days, no one can stop him. In his mind, there is nothing he cannot do. He is liable to fly to Caracas, take a car to Miraflores Palace, and demand that Chávez meet him on the front lawn to settle this like men." She examined her empty glass. "When he's down, he is a different person. He lies in bed for weeks until he smells. Won't get up for anything, not even to take a bath. His last bout started around Christmas."

"How is he feeling now?" I said.

"Emperor of the world." Iris looked at my glass. "You haven't had any wine," she said. "Wait right there." She stood and walked to the kitchen.

I sat back on the sofa. A few moments later Iris returned with the open bottle of wine. She refilled her glass.

"You need to drink so I can give you some more," she said, sitting back. "I make sure Benny takes his medicine and sees the doctor." She had a long drink. "His father pays for the treatment. He comes twice a year to see us and take care of business."

"He works with Benny?"

"Of course not. His father has condos, bank accounts, too. Everybody with two cents in Venezuela keeps a bank account in Miami."

"What about Benny's real estate business?" I asked her.

"Benny's clients are his great-aunt, who has some swampland in the northwest rife with Colombian guerrillas, and his mother, who inherited a small island so close to Guyana that it may not be Venezuelan territory. Money doesn't interest him, though. Neither does sex, from what I can tell," she said into her glass.

"Does he have any hobbies?" I said.

Iris put her glass on the table. She stood and waved for me to follow her to the second bedroom. The room was bare except for two metal filing cabinets and an old desk. Books, newspapers, and magazines were arranged in piles on the floor around the desk. Iris moved close to me. I could smell the wine on her breath.

"This is the kind of stuff Benny reads lately," she said, picking up a book and tapping the cover. "He stays up all night taking notes. Whatever he writes, he keeps locked in there," she said, pointing at the filing cabinets. I picked up another book from one of the piles. It was a how-to manual on staging a coup d'état, a small paperback with a gray cover and black letters, published by some think tank in California.

"Is he serious?" I asked.

"Of course not. Benny's a dabbler. A dreamer and dilettante. Impotent, too."

I put the book down, picked up a magazine, and pretended to flip through the pages.

"They say it's all the drugs he takes. I've tried everything, but it's no good. Sometimes I wonder if it's me." Iris picked up a copy of *El Nacional* dated last week. "This is his father," she said, tapping the front page. A picture showed a white-haired old man standing at a podium, mouth open, index finger in the air. Above the picture was the headline "Former Senator to Lead March Demanding Chávez Resign."

"Benny wants to be there," Iris said. Then she opened the bottom drawer of the desk and pulled out a passport. "This is Benny's. I would like you to keep it for me. No matter what happens, don't tell him that you have it."

I started to speak.

"Please," she said, taking my forearm.

Someone was slipping a key into the front door lock.

"Take it." Iris pushed the passport against my shirt and stepped out of the room. Benny was yelling something from the other side of the front door. I thought about putting the passport back in the drawer or even leaving it on the desk, when Benny pounded on the door and yelled Iris's name. So I slipped the passport into a pocket and hurried to the living room.

Iris motioned me to sit on the sofa. I picked up the photo album and opened it. Benny pounded on the door again.

"Just a minute," Iris called out, unlocking the door. Benny walked in with several large paper bags.

"Why the hell did you put the night lock on?" he said, placing the bags on the kitchen counter.

"Habit, I guess. I wasn't thinking."

"You weren't thinking?"

Iris said nothing.

"Is that also why you are practically naked, because you weren't thinking?" Benny said. One of the bags tipped over. At least a half dozen plastic bottles rolled over the counter and fell to the floor. They looked like chemical bottles—brown plastic, white label. Liquid swished inside as they rolled. Benny rushed to pick them up. He put them back in the bag and turned to me.

"Pests," he said.

I nodded and looked down at the photo album across my lap. When I looked up again, Benny was standing in front of me.

"I see Iris gave you her portfolio. She does that with everybody. Don't think that you're special."

Benny turned his head to get a better look at the album and squinted. He smelled of stale sweat, as if he'd been out all morning in the sun.

"I found Iris a photographer on South Beach to update her portfolio. Top-notch guy. Works with all the models." Then louder, so Iris could hear him, he said, "*Mi amor*, what is your photographer's name?"

Iris noisily uncorked another bottle in the kitchen.

Benny continued to talk while I looked at the pictures. There were close-ups of Iris smiling, then serious. Iris wearing a mink coat, a bikini, a white dress, carrying a parasol, like something by Monet.

Iris returned from the kitchen with a new bottle and another glass filled with wine. Benny took the glass and drank half of it in one gulp. I wondered if the wine would react with whatever drugs he had taken that day.

"Iris may not be nineteen anymore," Benny said, "but she is still beautiful." He tried to kiss her cheek.

"Careful, you made me spill some." She refilled her own glass.

I turned the page. There was Iris smiling over her shoulder and her bare back; another one of her crossing her arms. Iris lying on a white fur rug, looking impish. And Iris on the beach naked. I closed the photo album. When I looked up, Benny was watching me.

"Very nice," I said, and stood to leave, making up some excuse, thanking them for the wine, leaving my glass, still full, on the table.

Benny followed me out. "I want to tell you something," he said. "You know, my wife likes to overdramatize things. She likes to create her own reality. I'm not saying she's crazy. Only that the world"—he opened his arms wide—"is not exciting enough for her, so she invents things."

Benny moved closer to me. His breath smelled acrid, like burnt coffee mixed with ammonia. I took a step back. The heel of my shoe hit the wall behind me.

"I want you to rest assured that she and I have an understanding," he said. "Do you know what I mean by that? An understanding?"

I wanted to give him the passport and even reached for it in my pocket, when he said, "Good," and patted the side of my arm. "It is important for you to know that." Benny stepped back to the middle of the hall. "On the other hand, you must not believe everything she says. Like with the portfolio. She thinks that she can go back to modeling and pick up where she left off ten years ago, before we were married. I don't want to discourage her, so I hired a photographer. What is wrong with that?" Then he moved in close again and grabbed my elbow hard. "She tells people that I'm crazy."

I let go of the passport and took my hand out of my pocket. There was no telling how he would react if I tried to give it back to him now.

"I know she tells people that," he said, squeezing my elbow. "I don't mind. It is one of her fantasies—the beautiful young wife who gave up a promising career as a model to care for her sick husband. People have told me. Iris *has* to be the center of attention."

"Look—" I said.

"Good." He cut me off. "I knew you were my friend." He winked and walked back to his apartment.

For the next few days, my life settled back into its old routine. I woke early, drank one cup of coffee, and walked five miles in the morning, before it got too hot. Afterward, I showered and worked at my desk. The money my mother left me when she died is enough to allow me to live modestly, but the extra cash comes in handy. At noon, I ate lunch. Wednesday afternoon, I ran my errands between 2:00 and 4:00, avoiding any lines at the cleaners or the bank. The rest of the week, I sat by the pool and read. This year I'm reading about the smallest countries in the world, from Andorra to Vatican City. Last year, it was Brazil, the year before that Japan. At 7:00, I made dinner. By 9:00, I was in bed. Even when I watched TV, I rarely stayed awake past 10:00.

People like Benny and Iris, who make public every quake and tremor of their lives, break the monotony. Being around them is like speeding through a red light. Lately, I take my time doing the laundry, hoping Iris will come in. Or I linger in the mailroom, paging through the free newspapers, takeout menus, and flyers stacked on the bench beneath the mailboxes, keeping an eye out for Benny.

Over the next two weeks the situation in Venezuela worsened. Snipers shot at anti-Chávez demonstrators. High-ranking military officers demanded publicly that Chávez resign. On Monday morning, I was coming back from my walk, out of the elevator, when I heard Benny screaming at Iris in their apartment.

"I know you have it!"

"No, I don't."

"Yes, you do."

"I do not."

Glass shattered. Iris screamed.

The judge appeared around the corner wearing a gray exercise suit and a terry-cloth headband. His face was dry and his cologne smelled sweet.

"Do you think he's hurting her?" he asked me. Iris screamed again. "I'm calling the police," he said, and walked away.

I knocked on Benny's door. Everything became quiet.

"Benny, it's me."

Nothing.

"Benny? Iris? Is everything all right? The judge is calling the police. You have got to be quiet." When Benny opened the door, he was breathing heavily and his ears were red. I saw no sign of Iris.

"Hi." Benny smiled. "What did you say before? I was watching a DVD. Incredible sound system. Those Japs sure know electronics."

"Iris was screaming."

"Iris? She's in her room. Do you want me to get her?"

I told him about the judge calling the police.

"But why? Look for yourself." Benny stepped aside. "Would you like to come in?"

I looked over his shoulder. Nothing seemed out of place.

"I hope everything's OK," I said.

"Why shouldn't it be?"

I returned to my apartment. A few minutes later, there was more shouting. This time it was Benny. I walked out. Iris stood sobbing in the hall. Benny was in handcuffs. Two police officers, one on each side, walked him to the elevator. Behind them were two security guards and another police officer.

"Is this what you wanted?" Benny yelled at Iris. "Is it?" He kept yelling until the elevator doors closed. The judge's wife came out and took Iris away. I stood in the hall and listened to her muffled cries. Then it was quiet again.

The knocking woke me later that night. I felt my way to the front door and peered through the peephole. Iris's head looked much bigger than the rest of her. When I opened the door, it took a second before my eyes adjusted to the fluorescent lights in the hallway. Iris wore a short blouse, low-cut beltless jeans, and gold lamé sandals.

"I can't sleep," she said.

I made a big deal about rubbing my eyes.

"Benny's in jail," she said. "I don't know what to do. He wants to fly to Caracas to join the demonstrations against Chávez."

"Then I suppose he'll need his passport," I said.

I had put Benny's passport away in the bedroom. I decided to give it to her; let her worry about it.

When I returned to the living room, Iris had closed the door, switched on a lamp, and sat on the sofa. Her bare feet were tucked under her.

"I want to talk," she said.

I sat in the chair opposite the sofa and tossed the passport on the coffee table. Iris covered her face with her hands, and her shoulders started to shake. I felt that I had to do something, so I sat next to her.

Iris leaned into me, slid down on the sofa, and lay her head on my shoulder. Her hair was wet and smelled of peaches. I took a deep breath and held it for a moment.

Iris turned and kissed me. Her eyes were puffy and red and her nose was moist. The next kiss was longer. The one after that longer still. Until, kiss after kiss, I lost myself in her hair and in the faint smell of lavender that came off with each piece of her clothing.

2.

The next day I woke much later than usual. Iris was gone. It was too hot to go walking, so I listened to a CD of Glenn Gould playing the Goldberg Variations. My heart ran fast. My mind was fixed on the previous night. Bach seemed the perfect antidote. The music was orderly and rational. There was emotion but no surprises. Around lunchtime I boiled some pasta and tossed it with butter and fresh basil. I opened a bottle of wine that I'd kept in the refrigerator for months and drank half of it before I fell asleep on the sofa.

Benny must have been released on bail because later I heard them arguing.

"Stop speaking so much trash," Benny yelled.

"I do not speak trash," Iris yelled back.

"Yes, you do speak trash."

The telephone rang, but they ignored it.

"You are the one who speaks trash."

"No, you are the one who speaks trash."

And so on.

Around 3:00, I left some shirts and pants at the cleaners and picked up a bottle of wine at the liquor store. After that, I went to a bookstore and browsed through the section on New Urbanism, oversized books with colored-pencil drawings of towers topped with pennants, like de Chirico, only with brighter colors and wood slats instead of stucco. Around 8:00, I went home, dropped three ice cubes in a glass, poured some wine, and sat to read. After a few pages, I lay on the sofa and fell asleep. It was almost 11:00 when the sound of fingernails tapping on the door woke me. Iris's face filled the lens of the peephole.

When I let her in, she put a finger on my lips and kissed me.

"Where's Benny?" I asked.

"Asleep," she said. "Took his medicine. Said he couldn't sleep last night. Well, he was in jail, wasn't he? Not like he was staying at the Ritz-Carlton. He'll sleep until the morning for sure."

"But what if he wakes up?"

"If he wakes up, he'll see that I'm gone. If it's morning, he'll think that I left to do errands." Iris kissed me again.

"What if he comes looking for you?"

"He doesn't care."

"How can he not care?"

"He doesn't, OK?" Iris let go of me and walked to the window. She took the glass of wine I poured for her but did not drink.

"Now I don't feel like it anymore," she said. "I thought you wanted me to stay with you again, but now I don't feel like it."

I tried to kiss her.

"No." She gave me the glass and walked out. I put the glass down and followed her into the hall, whispering her name, trying to get her attention.

"Iris, stop!"

She walked into the darkness of her apartment and left the door open behind her. It wasn't like I weighed my options—go home, sleep, wake, walk, read, eat, and sleep again. I could do that. Or I could follow Iris.

I stepped inside. The front door closed behind me. My eyes were not yet adjusted to the dark. Everywhere I looked, I saw the ghost of the hallway lights. Someone was moving all around me.

I stretched one arm out but felt nothing. Benny was snoring in the bedroom. Their place had the same layout as mine. If the snoring came from my right, then all I had to do was—what?

I put both arms out and looked for the front door. Iris took my hands and brought them against her face, the curve of her waist, behind her back. She was naked. Then she kissed me. We kneeled and continued kissing, Iris moving my hands over different parts of her body. Finally, I lay on the carpet, Iris above me, just enough light coming in through the blinds now that I could make out the way her hair fell over her shoulders.

Iris pushed me out before the sun rose. I went home and fell into bed with my clothes on. When I woke, the sun was high. The surface of the bay shone pale green nearby and a hazy blue farther out. The palm trees shook in the breeze. Below my window, by the swimming pool, a man and a woman slept on chaises longues. A young girl lay on the other side of the pool with a cell phone pressed to her ear. I thought a swim would clear my mind.

The pool was quiet and the water was warm and pleasant. I swam from end to end and tried to think my way through this. I understood now what Benny meant when he said that they had an understanding. Sure. Benny was impotent. Wasn't that one of the first things Iris told me? He had his politics and his fantasies; she had her occasional affairs. It made sense, but I wondered how often she did this. Once a year? Every few months? Was it a regular thing or an occasional respite from the ups and downs of Benny's emotional life? Maybe Iris would come by for a few nights, even a few weeks, but eventually she would stop, her marriage to Benny intact.

After my swim, I found him waiting for me in the hall.

"Where?" Benny said, motioning with his hands. "I know you have my passport."

"I never wanted it in the first place, but—"

"Do you know that I spent a night in jail because you took my passport?"

"Now, wait a second—"

"You take my passport. I go nuts looking for it. I ask Iris. She acts dumb, so I lose my temper. That television judge calls the cops. And I'm dragged off to jail to spend the night with winos and petty criminals. I thought you were my friend."

I went inside and found the passport. Benny waited for me in the hall. He took it and walked off without looking at me.

That evening, I was finishing my dinner when Iris arrived. She looked very happy.

"Papa says we can play tonight." She kissed me.

"Where is Benny now?"

"Home." She walked to the windows and looked out on the dark bay.

"Does he know you're here?"

"Why are you so concerned with Benny? All you do is ask me about him."

"Does he know?"

"He is locked up in his room," she said, turning around to face me. "Wouldn't answer me when I spoke to him."

"Aren't you worried?"

"Why? He can't get into any trouble so long as he stays there."

Iris spent the night with me.

The next morning was Friday. I found the table set for breakfast and Iris in the kitchen. She moved from the stove to the refrigerator, put the dirty pans in the sink and ran water over them. I couldn't stop looking at her.

Around 5:00 that afternoon, she dressed. I asked her when she would be back. "Soon," she said, kissing the tip of her finger and placing it against my lips.

After she left, I watched a couple of old movies on TV until I fell asleep. When I woke, it was 3:00 in the morning. Outside, the bay was black, except for the trembling lights it reflected. I went to the kitchen and started putting the pans, dishes, and cups in the dishwasher, when a loud thump shook the apartment and made all the glasses rattle. It sounded as if someone had jumped off a chair and landed barefoot on the floor in the condo above me, except that the thump was followed by an echo that expanded beyond the city and the bay, like an explosion. Everything was quiet for a couple of minutes. Then sirens gradually filled the quiet.

The consulate, I thought.

Benny.

I dressed and went out. All the security guards in the building were in the lobby. No one knew what had happened.

I went outside and ran toward the consulate. There were fire trucks, ambulances, and police cars, their rotating red and blue lights skimming across the dark faces of the surrounding buildings. The blast had torn a hole, three stories high, through the building where the consulate used to be. The fountain was still working, its brass rods bent in anger, shooting jets of water over sheets of papers floating down to the street.

I went back and banged on Iris's door with the side of my fist. The judge appeared from around the corner wearing a robe over his pajamas. The lines in his face looked deeper.

"That explosion," I told him, excitedly. "It was the Venezuelan consulate."

The judge said nothing.

"I think Benny had something to do with it."

"Didn't you watch the evening news? Their president," the judge said, jamming his thumb in the air, "resigned yesterday morning. There was a coup or something. You know the kind of tomfoolery that goes on in those countries."

"He blew it up," I said. "He's been planning it for weeks."

"Benny's not here. He asked me to keep an eye on their place. On his *wife* too." The judge fixed his eyes on me and moved closer. "Listen to me," he said. "It's none of my business, but you seem like a reasonable guy."

I started to talk, but he would have none of it.

"No, you listen to me. I know you've been seeing that woman. Yup. We've seen and heard it all. Her sneaking over to your place in the middle of the night. Her husband waiting for you to get back. Maybe they're hip. Maybe they're swingers. You know that term? I don't suppose you use it anymore. I don't care. I do care about my peace and quiet. You know what I mean? I won't hesitate to call the cops on you too, if I need to. *Comprende?*"

The judge disappeared around the corner.

I did not go back to sleep. Later that morning, I read that Chávez had resigned the presidency but was already back in power. Local stations carried stories about the explosion at the consulate. Some thought it was the work of the anti-Chávez people, others that the Chavistas themselves had done it. No one mentioned any suspects.

Several times during the day, I walked out of my apartment and down the hall looking for any sign of Benny and Iris. I knocked on their door, hoping not to attract the judge's attention. Just because I'd done nothing illegal didn't mean he couldn't call security and accuse me of disturbing the peace.

In the evening, I tried their door again. This time Iris answered.

"You've heard?"

She nodded.

"What about Benny?"

"Benny is in the hospital, under observation."

"For what?"

"What do you think he's in the hospital for?"

I imagined the judge, ear pressed against his door, listening to us, so I spoke softly. "What do you plan to do?" I said.

"I will go to the hospital and see him later today. I will take care of him, do what I can to make sure he is not too uncomfortable. It's what I'm supposed to do."

"If there's anything—?"

"Thank you. I'll tell him you came by." She started to close the door. I held it with my hand.

"Iris?"

"Go home."

"What about us?"

"What *about* us? You and I had sex. That's all. Now my husband needs me."

"Benny told me about your understanding."

"Our what?"

"Your understanding. He told me it was fine. You know, it's OK if we—"

"You should not believe everything Benny tells you," she said. "It is bad for him. Now I would appreciate it if you left me and my husband alone."

Iris looked through me at the wall. I stepped back and let her close the door.

3.

I never saw them again. Waiting for the elevator one morning, the judge's wife told me that Iris and Benny were back in Caracas, taking care of his father, who had suffered a heart attack when he was arrested during the coup, along with most of the opposition leaders. Soon after that, their condo was sold to a young couple with a baby.

Benny's father died the next summer. His picture appeared on the Web sites of both *El Universal* and *El Nacional*. One paper showed the family standing around the grave. Benny wore a dark suit and tie and was caught squinting at the sky. Iris stood next to him, holding his hand. She wore a black dress, a hat, and large sunglasses. The caption under the picture identified Benny as a son of the one-time presidential aspirant; Iris as his wife and a finalist for the title of Miss Venezuela 1992. I printed the picture and saved it in a drawer. Every so often, I take the picture out and look at it for a long time, much longer than I would have predicted.

Faith

Trip says, "Hey, Irv, know what this morning felt like?"

"I know what it felt like for me," Irv says. "And I have a good idea what it felt like for the station."

Miami television news anchor Trip Perez and his lawyer, Irv Heller, stand in an art gallery on Lincoln Road, inside a refrigerator the size of a large closet. In the center is a sculpture, six gallons of the artist's bodily fluids frozen into the shape of a man in an upright anatomical pose, arms slightly out, palms facing forward.

"It felt like high school all over again," Trip says. "My buddies and I stayed out all night. It's kind of embarrassing to talk about it, but I can tell you. Attorney-client privilege, right?"

Irv holds a packet of gum, unwraps one, and bends it into his mouth. He balls up the wrapper and shoves it back into his pant pocket along with the rest.

"Just don't tell me you're gonna kill someone on camera for the ratings."

"That hurt, Irv. Right here." Trip taps his chest. His breath is visible in the freezing air.

"That was what, twenty-five years ago?" Irv says.

"Twenty. My mother was dead by then."

"Sorry to hear. What'd she die of?"

"Cancer."

Trip tugs the cuffs of his shirtsleeves. He looks trim and fit in a blue suit. Irv holds his coat over his shoulder, like a politician. His shirt is wrinkled, the tails bunched into his pants. A dab of wasabi adorns a pant leg.

"So whad'you do that's so embarrassing?" Irv says.

"Broke into houses. People we knew were out of town. Spent the night drinking their liquor. Lived off the adrenaline."

"I'll bet."

"Never did drugs. Never smoked."

Irv stuffs another stick of gum into his mouth. He offers one to Trip, who shakes his head. Trip says, "This morning, at the table, negotiating, felt something like that. Pure adrenaline."

"You made out like a bandit, Trip. Top-paid anchor in Miami. Control over the content of the show."

"I just have a say."

"A big say. And you're what? Thirty-five? Keep it up for a year or two, and from here it's on to the networks and seven figures."

Trip tightens his hands into fists.

"What I want to know," Irv says, "is what you see in this popsicle." He points his last stick of gum at the sculpture, before stuffing it in his mouth.

"Think of it as an investment," Trip says. "You know how much Saatchi paid for the early Damien Hirsts? Know what they're going for now?"

"So long as you're happy, I guess."

Trip walks around the sculpture. Crouches. He places the tips of his fingers on the cold floor.

"I'm going to take it," he says, standing.

"Does this thing have a name, or don't they do that anymore?"

"It's called *Ecce homo,* which means, my dear counselor, 'Behold,

man!'" Trip says, lifting an open hand in the direction of the sculpture. He says, "When I was a boy my father gave me a plastic model
that looked like this. It was called the Human Man or the Human
Body. He wanted me to be a doctor. Can you imagine me a doctor?"

"You're making more money than any doctor," Irv says.

"My brother's a surgeon."

"Your father's got to be proud of you."

Trip reaches out to touch the sculpture but stops short. "I think he
wants to be. That counts. Doesn't it?"

It is the time of year when refugees from Haiti and Cuba wash up on
the beaches of Miami. Nine months ago, Trip and his crew were the
first to get helicopter footage of Haitians running down the causeway
at rush hour, dodging cars and the police. They were also the first to
report—and only station to show—a corpse decomposing on South
Beach next to a powder blue wooden boat with the name *Ange de Dieu*
crudely painted in white on the stern. When Trip exhausted that
story, he interviewed local officials about the impact that finding a
corpse on the beach would have on tourism. Then he flew with a
cameraman to Europe and interviewed tour operators in Berlin,
Milan, Madrid, and London. He showed each tour operator eight-by-
ten color glossies of the corpse, the camera focused tight on their
faces, *60 Minutes*—style. But this year, with the coast guard on alert,
the beaches and causeways are quiet.

Like every weekday morning, Trip and his team meet in a long
conference room at the station to discuss the stories they will work
on that day.

"What do we have?" Trip says.

It is Tuesday morning. He sits at the head of a white formica table
stained with coffee cup rings. Reporter Jennifer McCue sits next
to him. At the other end is the news director, Tony Reggio. Walter
the weatherman, Harry the sports reporter, and Kharma Dayes, the
celebrity reporter, take the remaining seats. The sun reflects on
the bay and creates an animated weave of light on the ceiling.

Walter stands to close the mini-blinds. The weave disappears.

Jennifer says, "Trip, we've got a woman who says she saw the Virgin Mary."

"Give me a break," Harry says.

Walter groans.

Kharma smiles like she does in the ads for her talk show. The ads appear on billboards and bus benches. *Real people. Real close,* the ads read.

Jennifer wonders if Kharma's teeth are real. She says, "She's from Honduras. Been here ten years. Hotel maid."

"Figures," Walter says.

"The meek shall inherit the earth, Walt. Go on, Jen," says Trip.

"Happened yesterday morning, 'round rush hour. She was waiting for the 24 bus on Brickell and Tenth."

"Did she say anything about the ad for my new show?" Kharma says.

"Said she saw the Virgin Mary on the side of an office building."

"Con-den-sa-tion," Harry says.

"Yup. Temperature, humidity. Conditions are perfect for that kind of phenomenon," Walter says.

"Yesterday's a long time ago," Trip says. "How'd you find out about it?"

"Ricardo from the mailroom. Heard it on Spanish-language radio."

"Now we're being scooped by *Rah*-dee-yoe *Cue-bahn*-noe?" Walter says. "Anybody else seen this phenomenon?"

"Yeah. And how do we know she's not making this up just to get on television?" Harry says.

"Because she was scared I was going to report her to the IRS," Jennifer says.

"You mean the INS," Walt says.

"She cried when she told me about it. She stopped talking, closed her eyes, and cried."

"What did you expect?" Harry says. "Most of these people are illiterate. The other day I was talking to my gardener—"

"Find the woman," Trip says. "Interview her, take her to that bus bench on Brickell or wherever this happened. Do whatever you need to do to protect her identity, if she's afraid of being deported."

"Why does Jenny get to do everything?" Kharma says. "I can be sympathetic."

"Because you don't speak any *español*, that's why," Walt says.

"I've been to a Cuban restaurant," she says. "I can read the menu."

"Get a shot of her pointing at the building," Trip says. "Try to get a shot of whatever it was she saw. Call the archbishop or someone in his office. They've got to have an official position on this kind of thing. It's not the first time this has happened."

"Yeah, like last year, when those people thought they saw the face of Jesus Christ in a big oil slick outside Dadeland Mall," Harry says.

"Let's try to wrap this up for the five o'clock," Trip says.

"Now I've heard everything," Walt says, tapping a pencil on the table.

"Do you wanna stop that? It's giving me a headache," Kharma says, rubbing her temples. Walt stops.

"You have something better, Walt?" Trip says. "What's today's forecast?"

"Partly sunny. High in the mid-nineties. Thirty percent chance of late-afternoon showers," Walter says, modulating his voice the way he does when he is on the air.

"Same as yesterday. Same as the day before. My vote goes to the Honduran lady and her apparition. How about you, Tony, what do you think?"

"It's your show, Trip," Reggio says, holding his hands up.

It is night and Trip is home. A tiny black cordless phone is wedged between his shoulder and his ear. He is half listening to his father as he makes himself a drink.

"Your brother called me today."

"Uh-huh."

"Do you know that he starts operating at five in the morning?"

Trips lays the phone on the bar. He pours Scotch into a tumbler and takes a drink. He switches on the speakerphone. His father's voice sounds small.

"Might as well have taken holy orders."

"Who should have taken holy orders?"

"I never said that. I said might as well have taken holy orders. Are you listening?"

"Yeah, I'm listening."

"Remember last Saturday? I told you about our lives being interrupted by Castro, what we went through to leave Cuba, to start again in Miami? You seemed so skeptical. Yet when I told the same story to your brother today, he was still sympathetic, even though I've told him the story many times."

"How about that. And we're both from the same mother and father." Trip takes the tumbler and drinks the last of the Scotch. He pours some more.

"The French call it déformation professionelle. *Your brother is trained to assume that his patients are telling him the truth, so why would he not assume that I too was telling him the truth? But you, you are trained for the opposite. You assume everyone is lying to you, that everyone has an agenda. ¿Alo?"*

"Still here," Trip says, leaning toward the phone.

"Do you know that patients your brother has not seen for years still send him cards at Christmas?"

Trip points a slim black remote control at a flat TV screen as big as the wall and plays the Haitian tapes.

Outside, tree branches creak. He presses Pause. The image on the screen freezes cleanly. He gulps his drink and lays the remote control on the bar, next to the phone.

He walks to the back of the house and listens to his father's voice fade, until he cannot hear it anymore. He turns on the outside lights and slides open the glass doors. A screen roof covers the patio and the pool. He looks up and makes out the trees swaying in the wind. He turns on the pool light. He flips another switch. There's the sound of gurgling followed by the swelling of a small mound of water bubbling in a corner of the pool before plunging down steps of coral rock, making the bottom go out of focus. He turns off the waterfall and the lights and goes back inside.

Two days later, during the noon broadcast, Jennifer McCue reports on a second sighting. Behind her is the office building.

JENNIFER: That's right, Trip. We have a camera pointed at the side of the building where another person told us today that he saw the Virgin Mary.

TRIP [*talking to the monitor*]: Now we have a second eyewitness?

JENNIFER: Right. The first sighting occurred around eight-thirty, eight forty-five Monday morning. That was the Honduran woman we interviewed Tuesday. Yesterday's sighting happened during rush hour at five-fifteen in the afternoon. We've been here since eleven this morning, but nothing's materialized yet.

TRIP: Well, it's still early, Jen. Hang in there. [*To the camera*] If anything does happen, though, you'll see it here first, live on *News-Now!* Thanks, Jenny.

JENNIFER: You betcha.

TRIP: Curiouser and curiouser. Walt, I hope you're not going to disappoint me with any rain materializing over the weekend.

WALT: Things are quiet weatherwise, Trip. But we are watching a storm in the Caribbean. Right about here. At seven o'clock this morning Tropical Storm Fay, as it was designated earlier today, was at latitude 18.5 north and longitude 83.4 west, or roughly 144 miles southwest of Grand Cayman. Wind speeds of 35 knots. A tropical storm warning for the Cayman Islands went into effect at ten A.M. So far Fay is moving north-northeast. Very slowly. But that could change, so make sure you stay tuned to *NewsNow!* for the latest. Trip?

TRIP [*laughing*]: Just make sure not to ruin the weekend, Walt.

WALT [*saluting and laughing along*]: Yessir. OK. Now, for the rest of your weather forecast.

· · ·

Later that afternoon, Reggio walks into Trip's office.

"It's not good, Trip. Marty almost burst an artery when he heard that you sent Jenny and a cameraman to camp outside that building and wait for the Virgin Mary to appear. You know, the archbishop's office called Marty."

"Jenny's left no less than five messages asking for an interview with him."

"Marty says he'll take care of it."

"No he won't. Marty thinks he can run a news show in Miami just because he got a degree in communication from some prairie state university. To Marty we're all *hisspanicks*." Trip leans forward in his chair. He says, "Remember when he wanted me to do a piece on ponchos last year? Ponchos? I asked him. Yeah, Marty said. *Hisspanick* raincoats. No one's ever worn a poncho in Miami, if you don't count the time Dan Rather flew down to do a story. By the way, any reason Marty can't pick up the phone and talk to me?"

"Trip, I know you and Marty have discussed this umpteen times—"

"Who's idea was it to cover the Haitian who washed up on South Beach? Marty said I couldn't show the body. He wanted to do on-cameras with INS guys; a bunch of talking heads in polyester uniforms. I mean, you say, *A Haitian refugee was found dead on South Beach this afternoon by shocked German and Italian tourists,* and nobody gives a fuck, except maybe the hotels and the chamber of commerce."

"Don't forget the tourists."

"Yeah, right. But I showed the body. We had everybody talking about it. About us too. CNN even did that story—'Has the Media Gone Too Far?'—with that lesbo grilling me about journalistic ethics. What ethics? This is ratings, man. This is market share. Am I out of line here?"

"I know, Trip," Reggio says. "I know all about it. I was there, remember?"

Trip leans back. He says, "Even our Web site went ballistic. And all we did was show a body puffed up and rotting on the beach."

"We were famous there, for a while. That's for sure."

"Face it, more people watch us now than any other news show in Miami. This Virgin Mary story's got the public by their—"

"Coe-*hoe*-neeze."

"Exactly."

Trip takes a sheaf of papers from his desk. He says, "You picking up a little Spanish?"

"Poe-*kee*-toe."

"Still dating that Cuban girl?"

"Seeh."

"Best meat in town."

Later that day, Trip Perez and his team sit on the set ready to broadcast. The *NewsNow!* logo flies across the monitors. The studio is filled with a *swoosh* sound, followed by urgent music. A man's voice announces the 5:00 news. Trip stretches his neck and swallows. A technician behind a camera waves three fingers. Two. One.

TRIP: Hello, everyone. This is *NewsNow!* Five o'clock edition. I'm Trip Perez. We told you we'd be the first to bring you a live picture of the apparition that's the buzz all over Miami, and here it is: What you're looking at are the windows of an office building on Brickell Avenue and Tenth Street. Now look closely. Appearing on the windows of this building, at least five stories high, the image of a woman wearing a shawl. Some people see the Virgin Mary. Others not so sure. One thing's certain, *NewsNow!*'s Jennifer McCue is there live right now. Jenny?

JENNIFER: That's right, Trip. It happened before rush hour. One moment this was just another office building. The next, the figure of a woman appears, drawing people on foot, slowing down rush-hour traffic. *NewsNow!* has brought you exclusive interviews with the two people, the only two, who've seen this apparition. Now here's a tape of the image itself as it materializes. Let's watch.

NewsNow! replays the tape several times before the end of the day. On Saturday, ABC and NBC air their own tapes. CNN and Fox send reporters to interview the crowd that has gathered in the parking lot next to the building. People hold rosaries, sit on plastic coolers, watch portable TVs, and listen to radios. A man sells tee shirts bearing a picture of the Virgin Mary. Someone unrolls a banner that reads PRAY THE ROSARY FOR PEACE ON EARTH. The sky darkens and a light rain falls.

2.

It is late Saturday afternoon. Trip's driving home. The top of his car is down. His cell phone rings. Caller ID says it's his father. Trip thinks, Don't answer, but he presses Send anyway and puts the phone to his ear.

"Did you change your mind about the live-in nurse?"

"I thought I made myself clear. There is a saying in Spanish that goes, Better to be alone than in bad company."

"I would never accuse you of needing anyone."

"I am having the time of my life. I do not have to shave or answer the door. I can stay in my pajamas the entire week if I want to. In any case, that is not why I called. I wanted to talk to you about that news report, the one about the Virgin Mary. I do not think it is right what you are doing."

"We report the facts. That's all."

"You are doing a lot more than that."

"We did not make up the fact that some people think they see the Virgin Mary when they look at the windows of an office building in downtown Miami. I think it's ludicrous. You may think it's ludicrous, but these people believe it."

"I can hear it in your voice. It is not right to ridicule people like that."

Trip's father coughs heavily.

"Are you OK?"

"Sí, coño." His father laughs. It sounds phlegmy. Trip hears the sound of ice cubes in a glass. His father says, *"Why don't you stop? If not for me, at least do it for the memory of your mother."*

A jeep cuts in front of Trip. He slams on his brakes and blows the horn hard. He speeds up and swerves around the jeep. "The memory of my mother? I remember my mother suddenly dead." He turns a corner sharply and shifts down.

"There is nothing we can do about that now. You can stop these reports of yours."

"I'm not going to do that." Trip changes gears again and accelerates.

"You should stop being so hardheaded. Your mother—"

Trip presses End and throws the phone against the passenger-side floor. When he looks up, he is coming up fast on a car that is stopped in his lane, lights blinking. He presses the brakes, but the road is wet and his car slides. He releases the brakes and turns sharply to the right. His car runs onto the grass and comes to a stop inches from the trunk of a royal palm.

Later, at home, Trip's housekeeper helps the caterers set up. Trip walks into his bedroom. The bed is unmade and Jennifer McCue lies under the sheets reading a magazine. The TV is on mute.

"What happened to you? Honey?" Jennifer gets up and hugs him. She is naked.

"I'll tell you about it later."

It is 8:00 now. Most of the guests have arrived. In a corner of the living room is a refrigerated plexiglass case containing *Ecce Homo*. A few guests stand around it, holding drinks, talking. The waterfall in the pool is running. A cellist and a pianist play Bach. A bartender mixes drinks in a shaker shaped like a mortar shell. Jennifer walks out the double doors that lead to the bedrooms without drawing any attention. Trip talks with Tonya, the twenty-nine-year-old wife of Sol Meyersohn, the seventy-three-year-old owner of the station. Next to Tonya is her friend Nikki. Trip looks at Tonya's breasts.

"Tonya, the word is you got those last year."

"He's trying to say that you have implants," Nikki says.

"I know what he's trying to say. Of course I have implants. Doesn't everybody?"

"Sol doesn't have implants," Trip says.

"Says who? He's got a pacemaker. He's had a hair transplant. And he's got one of those things in his stomach that he presses to make his penis pop up like a jack-in-the-box."

Trip reddens.

"This is a first. Trip Perez blushing. Did I make you blush, baby? How else do you think he and I, you know?"

Sol Meyersohn walks up behind the girls and takes their arms. He wears large gold-rimmed sunglasses with peach-tinted lenses.

"You keeping my girls company, Trip?"

"Yes, sir. Just trying to be a good host."

"Well, you're the best. Lovely music. A bartender that's generous with the drinks. And the view. Have you seen the view?"

"You're not supposed to be looking at the girls, Sol," Tonya says.

"Say, what's the scoop on the Virgin Mary story?" Sol says. "You've got Marty real worried."

"Sol, you promised," Tonya says. "No business tonight."

"This isn't business. It's current affairs. You might learn something. Trip?"

"I'm getting another drink," Tonya says. "Nikki, you coming with me?"

"Aren't you going to offer to get anything for young Trip and me?"

"Young Trip and old Sol can get their own drinks."

"Must be that time," Sol says. "You know, there's a lot to be said for postmenopausal women. You were saying, Trip?"

"It's Marty's job to be cautious," Trip says. "It's mine to be audacious."

"Fancy word there. I hate dictionaries."

"Risk taker, courageous, brash."

"I've never been afraid of a little controversy. Hell, we make our living pissing people off, but the archbishop just gave an interview to CNN. You know that, right?"

Trip shakes his head.

"Yeah, he gave the interview to that woman—?"

"It's not the first time she's had it in for me. Calls me a living example of everything that can go wrong with television news."

"Her I don't care about. Well, actually I do. The more she rants about our little operation here, the more people are interested in it. That's why we recognized your contribution and gave you a significant raise when your contract came up for negotiation. I thought I saw your lawyer walking around here."

"I appreciate it."

"Don't mention it. I'm not supposed to tell you this, but poor Walt over there is making less this time around. Not his fault, I suppose. Unless there's a hurricane bearing down on us, people don't much care whether it's going to be partly cloudy or partly sunny. Hell, Trip, I know you work hard. I just don't like the archbishop going on national television and telling the world that he thinks you made up this story for the ratings."

"The archbishop does not run anything."

"You're absolutely right. But guess who'll answer the phone when the archbishop decides to put in a call to someone who has some real power. This is me talking, that's all."

"If the archbishop's so mad at us, why didn't he talk to me first? We're not the only ones covering the story."

"That's true, technically, but look at how everybody else is covering it. To them it's a story about the way we cover stories. Like saying, They're crazy down there in Miami. That's not responsible broadcast journalism. That's what that woman said. She even ran the Haitian tape."

"You won't be so upset about this when our ratings shoot through the roof."

"You know, if you weren't you I'd fire your ass for saying that. I don't want you to get us into something that has the potential of spinning out of control. Don't forget the mayor's a devout Catholic. Took a goddamn pilgrimage last year. Didn't know people still did that sort of thing. Sounds medieval to me, but what do I know."

"I hope the mayor does jump in, like Giuliani and the elephant crap painting. All they'll do is breathe a few more days of life into this story. In fact, I'll call him for an interview."

"Fine by me. Better yet, why don't you give Kharma a part of this? She could use the exposure. Her show's not doing too good."

"Then can you please get Marty off my back?"

"Trip, I just own the station. I don't get involved with the newsroom. Wouldn't look right. Say, I heard you bought a sculpture. Where is it?"

They walk to the corner and stand before the plexiglass case.

Tonya and Nikki meet them with drinks for everybody.

"We decided to be nice and get you drinks, after all," Tonya says.

Walter walks up. In his broadcast voice he says, "Trip, you keeping a corpse?" Then to the girls he says, "*Oh*-lah. *Hel*-lo."

Tonya and Nikki ignore him.

Trip says, "Tonya, Nikki, you know Walt? Walt, Nikki. Tonya is Mrs. Meyersohn."

"Jeez, I didn't know it was possible. Sorry, Mr. Meyersohn, I meant—"

"You don't have to explain a thing, Walter the Weatherman," Sol says. "So what do you think of young Trip's audacious purchase?"

"This thing here? I'm a landscape man myself," Walt says.

"I always thought of you as someone who looks at the big picture," Sol says.

"That's what weather is. By the way, I was, well, wondering if we could talk about the coming year. I have some ideas."

"I hate talking business when I'm enjoying myself. Right, Trip?"

"Right you are, Sol."

"By the way, what's the deal with Fay?" Sol asks.

Walt looks relieved. "Storm's strengthening. Made landfall in western Cuba. Could be veering our way. We should be under a hurricane watch by now."

"So what can we expect tomorrow?"

"Overcast skies with occasional wind gusts, precipitation, even some thunderstorm activity later in the day."

"Some what?"

"Rain."

"Why didn't you just say so?"

"A lot depends on whether the storm veers our way or heads north into the Gulf."

"What about all those people waiting for the Virgin Mary to reappear?" Tonya asks.

"They're gonna get wet. Gee, I need a refill," Walt says. "Anybody coming with me?"

The rest of the evening, Trip's guests talk about the storm and the crowd waiting for the next apparition. The crowd is estimated to be several thousand. A few guests make it to Trip's media room and switch on the wall-sized TV screen. Others follow. An old man announces on Spanish-language cable television that he will lead the rosary at noon tomorrow, Sunday. Trip tells his guests that Kharma Dayes of his team will report it live. Jennifer McCue suffers a coughing fit. A woman pats Jennifer on the back until she recovers, red-faced.

It is almost 1:00 in the morning when the maid and the caterers finish cleaning. Jennifer and Trip are in the bedroom. She is screaming at Trip about letting Kharma follow up on the story. Trip tries to embrace her, but she runs to the bathroom and locks the door. Trip stands outside the door. "Jen," he calls out. "Don't be like that." "Go away!" Jennifer shouts. "You're fucking her, aren't you?" she says. "How can you say that?" Trip says. He undresses and lies in bed. "Jen," he calls out from the bed. He draws a pillow over his eyes. Outside, the gusts become stronger. The sound of raindrops hitting the windowpanes is the last thing he hears before falling asleep.

3.

Sheets of rain rap against the bedroom windows. A tree branch snaps and hits the roof, waking Trip.

He slips out of bed and walks to the bathroom, where he splashes water on his face and looks in the mirror at the corner of his eyes and at his neck. Several times he smiles, pulling tight the muscles of his face and neck, before relaxing them. Then he walks out of the bathroom, down the hall, into the living room, through the sliding glass door, and out to the pool. The surface of the water is rippled by rain and gusts of wind. The trees above him sway like underwater plants.

On his way back to the bedroom, the door to the study is open. Jennifer lies on the sofa, eyes closed. Trip kneels next to her.

"What are you doing?" she asks.

"I thought you were asleep." He tries to kiss her.

"Don't," she says.

"Jenny, please. You know how I feel about you."

She yawns and rubs her eyes. "As a matter of fact," she says, "I don't know how you feel about me."

"How can you say that?" Trip says. He strokes her face, but she stops him. "Giving it to Kharma was old man Meyersohn's idea," he says. "Her show's not doing too well. It's just for today." He kisses Jennifer's cheek. "It's still your story," he says.

Jennifer takes his face in both hands and pushes him back.

"Tell me that you love me," she says. "I want to hear you say it."

Trip smiles. He caresses her cheek with his fingers. And he nods, once.

Trip and Jennifer watch the noon report lying in bed. Kharma Dayes wears a blue windbreaker with the *NewsNow!* logo. Her blond hair is pinned away from her face. Her teeth are resplendent in the television lights. The camera turns a few degrees and zooms in on the crowd behind her. Thousands of people wait under umbrellas. They wave homemade banners and pictures of the Virgin Mary. The camera pans slowly. A temporary stage slides into view. The stage is at the base of the glass wall where the apparitions were seen. Spotlights shine on a small old man dressed in black who stands in the center of the stage in front of a microphone. Two young men with matching black tee shirts use both hands to steady umbrellas over the old man. His voice echoes in the open space, against the surrounding buildings, but Kharma does not stop talking so it is impossible to understand him.

The camera pans past the stage. Barricades block the street. People fill the screen as far as the camera can see. Kharma describes the crowd as this multitude, this teeming sea of humanity. Trip groans and changes the channel.

"Come on," Jennifer says, "I wanna see her make an ass of herself."

Trip changes the channel back to *NewsNow!* Kharma has stopped talking.

"Good," Trip says, "she shut up."

Tight shot on the old man. The frame shakes. He leads the crowd in praying the rosary. The crowd's response sounds like bees buzzing. Trip tries to make out the words, but he cannot.

Just as at his mother's wake, twenty-one years before, when a man wearing street clothes walked into the room, shook his father's hand, and said he was the priest. Trip had never seen a priest out of uniform or one who looked so young. He thought his father should ask to see some identification, but his father had already told him not to say anything. He was never to tell anyone what had happened.

The priest knelt in front of the open casket. No one moved or spoke until he stood and made the sign of the cross in the air in front of him. He led the group in prayers that Trip recognized from grade school. Then the priest announced that he would lead everyone in saying the rosary. And as Trip listened to the priest say the words, then the women repeat them, he stared at his mother's face, hoping for a reaction. Something had to happen, he thought, with this many people praying for one thing, like a magnifying glass focusing the rays of the sun on a dried leaf. Hold the piercing white dot of light long enough and the leaf would smolder, fold over, and catch fire.

His mother had been fine until a few months before when she started to have headaches and see flashes of light. Her doctor told her that she had cancer and that it had spread to her brain, her back, and legs. His father became angry and took it out by accusing Trip of leaving the butter out, the lights on, drinking too many sodas. After school, Trip and his mother talked for hours, until it was time to make dinner. But once his father came home, Trip went into his room. It was November and the air had cooled enough for them to turn the air conditioner off and open the windows. At night, he lay in bed, imagining that the sound of traffic was really waves that didn't quite break on a beach.

One afternoon, Trip came home to find his mother taking her clothes out of the closet and tossing them on the bed. She put them in grocery bags. Together they drove to a church where she left them, like an offering, underneath the statue of Saint Jude. On another afternoon, he coaxed her into playing the piano, an old black upright that needed tuning. He watched her play uncertainly, her hands marked by pinpricks of dried blood and islands of pink skin where adhesive bandages had been pulled off.

Then she left for the hospital. "Tests," his father told him. "Don't worry about it. We have everything under control," his brother said. But after a week in the hospital, she returned looking worse.

Then one day, Trip came home from school and found the door to his parents' room closed. No one answered when he knocked. She's sleeping, he thought.

He went back to his room, tossed his book bag into a corner, and put on his headphones to listen to music. His watch read 3:20.

At 4:55, he took off his headphones and walked into the living room. His brother had not yet returned from the library and the door to his parents' room was still closed.

He knocked again. This time, when there was no answer, he opened it.

On the bed was his mother's body, naked, one arm hanging off the side, two empty bottles of painkillers next to her.

Trip does not remember how long he stood there. When they found him, he was sitting in the doorframe, hugging his knees.

The night of the wake, Trip lay in bed listening to the traffic. He may have fallen asleep. He may have dreamt everything that happened, but he prefers to believe that it did happen, that his mother came into his room and stood next to his bed, much younger and very bright. He sat up, startled, but she did not move. He heard himself ask her, "Why?"

She closed her eyes and opened them and shrugged. Then she did not move again.

The next day, the sun was high and the world seemed wrong for a burial. The light was everywhere, making him feel guilty.

At the cemetery, a man from the funeral home led a ceremony of sorts. The men stood, their hands clasped in front of them. The women dabbed their eyes with paper tissues. A motor whirred and the casket descended halfway into the ground before it stopped. The man from the funeral home gave Trip and his brother each a red rose. His brother, in a neat dark blue blazer, bow tie, and gray trousers, tossed the rose into the grave. Trip did nothing. His father elbowed him, but Trip closed his eyes and held them shut until he heard the motor whir again, longer this time.

Twenty-one years later, Trip hears it over the TV, the motor lowering his mother's casket into the ground. He hears the priest leading the rosary, Kharma talking, and Jennifer saying, "Honey? Honey, what's the matter?"

What happens next happens quickly. The phone rings. Jennifer answers it.

Marty says, "Where's Trip, Jennifer?"

"He can't come to the phone. May I take a message?"

"Get him right now. Because if you don't, if I have to watch one more minute of this airhead, I am going to drive downtown and personally shut everything down. If it weren't for old man Meyersohn, I would've done that days ago."

Trip takes the phone and shouts into it. When he hangs up, he tells Jennifer to get dressed. Less than an hour later, they are at the station.

Trip goes to confront Marty, but the door to his office is closed and locked. Marty will not come out.

Reggio tells Trip that Marty wants to show people preparing for the storm, now a hurricane, that is expected to hit overnight. He sends Kharma and Jennifer out with two crews. Trip is ordered to stand by, ready to broadcast. "Marty's idea," Reggio says, shrugging.

Every hour, Walter reports on the position and strength of Hurricane Fay. Kharma and Jennifer report live from places like hardware stores, supermarkets, and gas stations. Jennifer asks a man with a cart full of groceries what he thinks about the storm. "What's there to think?" the man says. "It's God's will."

The wind tears down power lines in parts of the city. Trip listens to a voice mail from his maid saying that she will spend the night with her sister.

Around 7:00, Marty orders coverage of the storm to preempt everything else, the programming to begin at 8:00. Reggio tells Trip to dress and man the desk. Kharma and her crew are set up to do on-cameras from a bar in the suburbs where people will be drinking all night. Jennifer rides in the back of a news truck toward South Beach. On the way there, she asks the driver to turn into the parking lot next to the building where earlier they had reported on the apparitions. The lot is empty and flooded. The building lights blur with each sheet of rain that falls against the truck windows. Then they drive on.

At 8:00, the words HURRICANE FAY appear across every monitor in the studio accompanied by the sound of punctuated music and howling wind. Trip sits alone at the desk. Walter stands in front of a blue background. Together they report on the hurricane. They go to Kharma. Behind her is a group of young people smiling, waving, and raising their glasses. They go to Jennifer, who stands wearing a cap and raincoat, holding a microphone, the waves breaking on the beach barely visible behind her.

Outside, winds gust to eighty miles an hour. Walter and Trip go through a checklist of last-minute things to do before the hurricane hits, which is now expected to occur at around 2:00 in the morning.

They reach the mayor by phone and interview him. "Everyone is on maximum-alert status for any emergency-type situation," the mayor says from his bunker.

Trip and Walter stay on the air until 6:00 in the morning. By then the hurricane has passed through the city and is heading northeast over the Atlantic.

The techs pat them on the back. Marty appears and shakes Trip's hand. Then they embrace, and everyone in the studio applauds.

Trip goes to his office, throws himself on the couch, and sleeps.

At 10:00, he wakes. He looks for Jennifer. A tech tells him that she went home.

Trip leaves the station. Outside, the winds buffet his car. The few traffic lights that work flash on and off. He sees only one other vehicle, a city truck.

Near his house, fallen trees lie on the street, and he has to drive around them. His house looks undamaged, though nothing happens when he clicks the garage door remote control.

Inside, Trip tries every switch. The power is out. From the family room, he looks through the sliding glass doors at the pool. A large tree branch tore through the screen enclosure and lies half-submerged like a rocket that has crashed nose-first.

He walks past the bar and into the living room. Light comes in through the windows and reflects on the marble floor. That's when he smells it.

In the corner is a dark puddle oozing out of the plexiglass enclosure. Trip buries his face in the crook of his elbow. He stands in the living room, looking at the corner, seeing nothing in particular.

Melancholy Guide
through the Country of Want

1.

Es tan corto el amor, y es tan largo el olvido.

—Pablo Neruda

It is the first Thursday of the month, around 5:00 in the afternoon, and Ugo asks his maid, Paola, to prepare his bath. Afterward, he dresses in a white shirt, a pair of gold ladybug cuff links, a blue tie with pink elephants, and a tailored gray suit of a conservative cut. He tucks a small white pocket square in the breast pocket of his coat, leaving just enough showing to suggest that its presence is almost an afterthought. You never want to look like you're trying. He recites the famous passage from Castiglione, *"Quella esser vera arte che non pare esser arte,"* marking each trochee by chopping at the air with an ivory shoehorn, which he then uses to slip his feet into a pair of black leather shoes.

He is buoyant, dressed for the wine and jazz cocktail at the museum of art, eager to sip oaky Chardonnay and tour the galleries.

He won't stay more than an hour. He does not want to overdo it. It is his first night out in almost two years.

After the museum, he will come home. Paola will have set out a crystal glass and carafe with mineral water on a silver tray atop the night table next to his bed. There will also be a bottle of aspirins and another of sleeping pills in case he needs them. She is good about details like that.

Paola is short and brown and dyes her hair the color of a new penny. Her arms are fat and her cheeks wide and flat. She uses the formal voice in Spanish when she addresses Ugo—*Sí, Don Ugo. Inmediatamente, señor*—and keeps her uniform starched and clean. In the afternoons, Ugo watches her nine-year-old son, Felipe, play in the garden. Every few weeks he buys the boy another book by Jules Verne, H. G. Wells, or Robert Louis Stevenson, even though he has never spied the boy reading. With each book, Paola ushers in her son to say "thank you." At least she is grateful. She is very handy too. She plastered the bullet holes in the bedroom wall and taped a plastic sheet over the shattered panes of the French doors leading to the balcony.

Paola is the fourth maid Ugo hired since old Mrs. Norcross died. The Norcrosses worked for Ugo's father when he was single in the early 1950s, his father and mother after they married at the end of that decade, his mother when his father disappeared a few years later, Ugo and his widowed mother for nineteen years, and finally Ugo alone, when his mother died of cancer thirteen years ago.

Then Mr. Norcross died, and Ugo told Mrs. Norcross that she could stay in the apartment over the garage where she and her husband had lived for decades. Ugo closed most of the two-story, twenty-four-room house. He limited himself to using one bedroom, a bath, and an adjacent sitting room upstairs, as well as the large library with the view of the bay on the first floor. He didn't need a live-in maid, he told Mrs. Norcross. He would hire someone to come in for a few hours. All she would have to do is supervise. But she said that idleness was the quickest way to the grave and she would never allow anyone else to do her job. Until the week before she left for the hospital, she kept his house in order, did his laundry, and cooked for him too.

After Mrs. Norcross died, Ugo's mail accumulated in his box. The newspapers, which only the Norcrosses had read, piled up next to the front gate, not far from the intercom.

2.

Es ella la que viene por la noche, sin que yo la llame,
sin que sepa de dónde sale.

—Juan Carlos Onetti

The pile of newspapers next to the front gate was the reason that Ugo's neighbor, Mrs. Bud Alvarez, formerly Mrs. Manny Lustgarten (as in *Dr.* Lustgarten, the cosmetic dentist who appears in those late-night infomercials), née Bettina Leahy (you've seen her late father's concrete mixers with the stupid green parrot logo going round and round), began to call on him daily and use a funny, singsong voice when she spoke over the intercom.

"It's me, Bettina. Are you alive in there?"

When she learned that Ugo lived without any staff, she occasionally sent her gardeners, three maids, and even food. Bettina—please don't call me Betty—was in her late twenties, lived in the house next to Ugo, and had recently divorced her plaintiff-attorney husband. Ugo protested all the attention she gave him and even offered to pay for the servants' time, but Bettina dismissed him. "Now that the divorce is final, I have nothing to do," she said. "I've decided to make you my hobby."

One weekend afternoon, Ugo lay next to the pool with a copy of Boethius, which he had taken from his library. He preferred to read the classics in their original Latin or Greek. He was reading the second page, a line that he translated as, "I became aware of a woman of incredible beauty," or maybe the more correct translation was "a woman of breathtaking appearance," not "beauty" exactly (he made a mental note to consult the Latin-English dictionary later), when he looked up from the small leather volume and saw Bettina walking toward him wearing a sheer dress, a bikini underneath, high heels, and sunglasses. Her black hair was tied in a bun on the top of her head. Behind her, her butler and a maid carried two trays. A third maid carried an ice chest.

"Hey there," Bettina sang out. "I was about to have lunch alfresco by the loggia next to my pool when I saw you sitting here by yourself."

Ugo stood. Bettina greeted him with a kiss on each cheek. Her perfume was bright and smelled of citrus. "I can't keep letting you do this," he said.

The butler directed the maids as they moved a wrought-iron table under the banyan tree, set a white tablecloth, dishes, silverware, and served the food.

Then Bettina shooed away her butler, and he, in turn, waved the maids out through the gate, closing it ceremoniously behind him.

She served Ugo slices of prosciutto and melon, tiny scoops of beluga on Melba toast, and a flute of very cold brut that made him squint. She moved her chair next to him. As he ate, she told him stories about her acquaintances—local politicians, basketball players, rap artists, plastic surgeons, people she had met through her ex-husband and who had stopped speaking to her after the divorce. "They weren't really my friends, anyway." Every so often, she put her hand on his forearm. She told him about the secret fetish of a TV anchor. "I'm not kidding, his girlfriend needed fifteen stitches. She called the cops on him, of course."

"Aren't you going to eat?"

"No one ever gained weight by sharing gossip." And she told him the never-proven rumor about the former wife of a famous restaurateur. "People say she killed him so she could marry the fast-food tycoon she's with now. It's too droll. I'm surprised you don't know them. You must not get out much." Then her butler appeared, opened the gate, and ceremoniously announced that the lady's presence was required at home.

"What is it?"

"It's Mr. Alvarez. When Tere answered the door, he burst inside. He claims that several objets d'art belong to him and he is piling them in his car."

"Call the police," Bettina said.

"They say it is a civil matter, ma'am."

"You left him alone in my house."

"Tere's there too."

Bettina sighed and stood. Ugo stood too. He watched her walk toward the gate carefully, so her heels would not get stuck in the gaps between the tiles.

Ugo did not see Bettina again for several days. The table remained as they left it, uneaten melon and prosciutto rotting in the sun. At night, a cat or maybe an opossum licked the caviar out of the shallow jar and ate the remaining fruit, even the rind. The wind blew an empty bottle and the bucket off the table, onto the tiles. The bucket and bottle rolled into the pool. By the third day, a cloud of flies darkened the table. By the fifth day, the flies were gone.

Years before, when Ugo's mother was alive, she told and retold him the story about his ancestors. They had sailed from southeast France in the early 1500s to settle on the Caribbean island of Gran Tortuga, which they called La Grande Tortue, an island so small, off the greater island of Hispaniola, that most maps omitted it, especially after World War II, when it became one of the world's best places to launder money. His ancestors founded the principal city on the island, Saint Michel, and built the port at one end of the harbor. They grew sugar cane, tobacco, and cocoa, and traded with the Dutch for tools, bolts of linen, and Protestant Bibles. When English privateers tried to invade the island in the late 1700s, his bearded ancestors defeated them and set fire to their ships. Those who survived were captured, tied to long wooden spits, and roasted alive over a boucan. A boucan, his mother explained, was a pit with burning charcoal that his ancestors used to cook the wild boars they hunted with muskets and arquebuses in the densely forested hills inland.

In gratitude for defending the island, the king of France bestowed upon his ancestors the titles of Comte de Saint Michel de la Tortue and Baron de l'Atalaye. The king gave them two-thirds of the island's arable land, so that even after the revolution of 1804 and the establishment of the republic, the steady succession of presidents were all handpicked by the family over late-night cognacs at the estate on the hilltop overlooking the harbor.

For 152 years, two parties, the Whites and the Blues, shared political power. While one party held the presidency for two terms, the other party held the majority in the National Assembly. All citizens over twenty-one were required to vote in every election, even if the outcome had been predetermined in private negotiations.

The system worked peacefully until 1940, when it was rumored that the presidential candidate for the Blues, one of the most popular men on the island, planned to question the legitimacy of the election, which would have gone to the White candidate, as it was that party's turn at incumbency. Intermediaries shuttled messages between power brokers, bribes were offered, but the Blue candidate did not waver. The crisis came to a sudden end one rainy evening when the candidate's driver lost control of his car and drove over a cliff, killing everyone inside, including the candidate.

By official decree, the blue and white flag of the republic flew at half-staff for three days. The Blue party fielded a substitute candidate, an aging poet with no political experience, and the election took place. Everyone agreed that the poet's concession speech was the epitome of elegance and style. And while his poems are largely forgotten, students in secondary schools still have to memorize the speech as part of the curriculum.

By 1950, Ugo's family owned all the sugar mills and the Banco San Rafael, the island's largest bank, with offices in New York and Geneva. During the world wars, they became the third-largest supplier of sugar to the United States, causing severe shortages locally. The cocktail named Bitter Dregs (a shot of light rum, ice, guava juice, and a dash of aromatic bitters) was created by Ugo's great-grandfather during one of those shortages.

The island was the second-most traveled spot in the Caribbean after Havana. New money built hotels and casinos. In 1956, Xavier Cugat's orchestra flew in to play two sets in the grand salon of the Hôtel Caraïbien to a standing-room-only crowd. Ugo's mother showed him the black-and-white picture of his father in a white dinner jacket sitting at a table with the maestro and a buxom blonde. His father was an executive in the family bank, which sponsored the event. He was not yet thirty, but already he was handling millions of dollars for the government at a time when a million dollars was enough to set you up for life, she said.

The new monied people launched the island's first television station and a second newspaper to compete with the establishment press. Matters that were once settled behind closed doors appeared on its front pages. Reporters competed to write the most scandalous story, and headlines tested the limits of good taste. Then someone discovered irregularities in the treasury. For twelve years, the government had wired tens of thousands of dollars each month to an account in the New York branch of the family bank. The account belonged to the Argus-Tortuga Engineering firm. The minister of the treasury, in the first live television interview of a government official, claimed that the money went to a prestigious firm of engineers who would design a hydroelectric plant in the hills, but no plans were discovered. The firm had only a post office box in Brooklyn, and the two men who were listed as signatories to the account were rumored to have fled to Panama.

The minister of the treasury was jailed and later released. The president was forced to resign and went into exile in Quito. Both newspapers ran front-page stories about the scandal and named the persons who were involved. Ugo's father fled to Miami. He had planned to make his way north by train to New York, sail to Europe, and settle in Paris to wait out the crisis, but that was before he met Ugo's mother.

It was the late fifties. Most English speakers in Miami pronounced the name of the city My-ah-mah, and the only time you heard Spanish spoken on the street was when Cuban Castro sympathizers gathered at the entrance of the Tivoli movie theater on Flagler Street and Eighth Avenue to collect donations for the revolutionaries, who were still in the hills then. Nobody locked his door at night. The Rat Pack flew in to sing at the Fontainebleau and the Eden Roc on Miami Beach. Ugo's mother worked *as a model for a couturier on Lincoln Road and dreamt about applying for a job as a stewardess with Pan American, seeing the world, and marrying a rich executive. "Imagine," she told Ugo once, "if I'd done that, I would have never met your father and you wouldn't exist."*

Ugo's mother and father met on a Friday evening. Another of the couturier models invited her to the Fontainebleau for drinks. They sat at a small table in the Boom-Boom Room where, instead of the Rat Pack, a Latin crooner sang boleros, accompanied by a four-man band. When Ugo's father came over to their table, she almost died. Those were her words, "I almost died. He was so handsome, I thought he was a movie star." The feeling was mutual, she told Ugo, because his father proposed to her before she had finished her second brandy Alexander.

When Ugo was four years old, his father went out alone on his yacht and did not return. The coast guard found the unmanned boat drifting north in the Gulf Stream. The last ten pages in the logbook and even the endpapers were filled with one word—noia, "boredom" in Italian—neatly printed in his father's hand.

Ugo's mother sold the yacht and kept the logbook, which Ugo found and hid when he was eight, along with a picture of his father taken when he was in his twenties, slipping the key into the door of an English roadster. His father looked slim in a linen jacket and pants. He wore loafers without socks. Every few years, Ugo took the logbook and the picture and examined them, as if they could tell him something.

Bettina Alvarez returned a week later and rang the doorbell. Ugo put down the book he was reading (Erasmus this time, on passion and reason) before he stood to answer.

"Let me in," Bettina said over the intercom. "We're celebrating."

"What are we celebrating?"

"You won't know that unless you let me in."

Ugo went to the front of the house and opened the door.

Bettina handed him two bottles of champagne. Her black hair was pulled away from her face by a shiny tortoiseshell band. She wore a short dress. Even in flat shoes, she was tall. "What were you doing?"

"I was reading."

"You'll go blind."

Ugo walked into a sitting room and showed Bettina to an old leather sofa. From a cabinet, he reached for two flute glasses. The rim of a glass struck the cabinet door as he took it down and rang in a clear, sustained note. He opened one of the bottles and poured the champagne.

"We are celebrating the fact that the judge entered a restraining order against my ex-husband," Bettina said. "He can't come anywhere near my house. If he does, all I have to do is call my attorney. Not only will he be found in contempt, the judge told him that she would personally call the bar and file a complaint against him."

Ugo nodded, though many of the words, used in this context, were new to him.

"You should have seen my ex-husband in court. He looked like he was going to pee in his pants. The great Bud Alvarez, with a silver tongue and gold-lined pockets, silenced and scared."

"Here's to your retraining order," Ugo said.

Bettina laughed into her glass. "You're cute." She drank the champagne in one gulp.

Ugo refilled her glass slowly. Her cell phone rang, a few bars of Chopin's "Marche funèbre."

"I can't believe this!" Bettina pulled her phone from a slit pocket in her dress. "Whad'you want?" She looked at Ugo and raised her index finger. "What part of the court order didn't you understand, you guava head? You want me to call Leona right now? You want me to ask her to find you in contempt?"

She sat straight and put both her feet on the floor.

"Fine, so it's the judge who finds you in contempt," she said, standing. "It's still Leona I'm calling. And *she* can get the judge to find you in contempt. And while she's at it, she can also get you to pay her attorney's fees, which I wouldn't be incurring if you weren't acting like a bona fide asshole."

Bettina threw the cell phone against the wall so hard that it broke into several pieces. One of its keys slid across the carpet and landed at Ugo's feet. She breathed deeply and closed her eyes.

"I'm in a safe place," she said under her breath. "I'm in a friendly place."

"I have some herbal tea that is supposed to be good for you. My mother brought it back from one of her trips. Would you prefer some of that?" Ugo asked her.

But she stayed quiet, her eyelids fluttering. When she opened them, she saw the pieces of her cell phone scattered on the carpet and the mark where the phone had struck the wall. She examined the mark closely. "I hope I didn't ruin the wallpaper. Did it come with the house?"

"It's always been there," Ugo said.

She ran her hand against the wall. A small piece of the wallpaper tore off.

Bettina sat again, close to Ugo. "I'm sorry about that," she said. "That was my ex-husband, but I guess you figured that out. It's just that he makes me so mad. It's bad enough that he still calls me, but it's like I can't get away from the man. His picture's everywhere—on buses, bus benches, the Yellow Pages. There's even a banner—'Alvarez Accident Attorneys,' it says—that streams behind a propeller plane that flies over downtown. His ad comes on at least fifty gazillion times every afternoon on all the TV channels, on radio too. 'Have you been seriously injured?' That's how the ad used to start. When he wasn't getting enough calls, he dropped the 'seriously.'"

"Are you sure you don't still have feelings for him, maybe?" Ugo asked.

"Buddy was a stage in my life. I'm over him. Besides, he's too jealous, a real nut case. He used to go through my purse. He had spyware installed on my computer. Every time I sent an e-mail, a copy of it went secretly to him."

"What was he so afraid of?"

"What do you think he was so afraid of? He thought I was going to cheat on him?"

"And did you?"

"You know, for such a polite little nerd who never gets out, you sure know how to ask a direct question. No, I never cheated on him. How could I? He tracked my every movement 24/7. He was jealous of everybody, even my girlfriends. Four of us went out to lunch once. These are girls I've known since high school, OK? What do you think he does? He calls my cell phone every fifteen minutes. 'Where are you? Who're you with? What're you doing?' The same three questions. Finally, I just turned the phone off. When I got home, all my clothes were gone. I never found out what he did with them, probably dumped them somewhere out of anger. His little temper tantrum cost him big-time, though, because I made him buy me a whole new wardrobe."

"So you came out all right."

"No I did not come out all right because no wardrobe is worth going through what I did. He made my life miserable."

"How long were you married?"

"Three years. I tried to make it work. I didn't want another divorce. My family gave me hell the first time around. You expect your own family to back you up, give you moral support, then they turn on you."

"I wouldn't know about that." Ugo stood and walked to the window. He separated two slats in the blinds and peered through the opening at the sunlit garden. "I have no brothers or sisters. My mother prohibited all contact with her own family and my father's family too."

Bettina walked behind Ugo and put her hand on his shoulder. "How odd."

"Not really. She hated my father's family because they rejected her, and she was ashamed of her own because they were poor."

"She told you that?"

"I overheard her."

"I've spent my entire life surrounded by people. I don't know what I would do without noise. This Bates Motel thing you have going on here is spooky. No offense. Listen, I'm doing all the talking here. The least you can do is top me off." She raised her glass. "More *shahm-pahn-nyuh,* if you please."

Ugo refilled her glass. Bettina took it and drank.

"I am really sorry about the wallpaper," she said, "Maybe I can find someone to repair it, paint it or something, make it look good as new."

"You needn't worry, no one is going to see it."

"I think I've had enough champagne. Do you mind if we sit by the pool? I need to look at the bay. It'll calm me down."

They left the champagne and glasses in the sitting room and walked through a long hall with dark oak paneling. On the walls were oil paintings, canvases with dollops of bright blues and yellows, hanging in thickly ornamented gold frames.

"Does your ex-husband want to go back with you?"

"No. Yes. I don't know. It doesn't matter. I told you I'm over him. I need to move on."

They turned into another hall. At the end was a door with a large window through which they could see the bay. Ugo opened the door to the patio and let her through. "Maybe you were never in love with him," he said. "I mean never really in love."

Bettina stopped. "What do you know about love?" She walked past Ugo and stepped outside.

The remains of their lunch from the previous week was on the table. Two plates and a glass were shattered on the tiles. One corner of the linen tablecloth was chewed and frayed. A chair lay overturned. Bettina walked to the edge of the pool and saw a bottle and the cooler at the bottom.

"You still don't have any staff?" she said.

"I haven't gotten around to it," Ugo said.

"You are truly a case. Don't move," Bettina said.

Within minutes, five maids came from her house and collected the plates and glasses, and they cleaned and put the iron furniture back in its place.

"Living like this is unnatural," Bettina said. "I'll find you a maid." Over the next few weeks, she called housekeeping services and interviewed the maids herself. The first maid she hired stole two pairs of cuff links and some silverware. The second maid sneaked her boyfriend in late at night. Ugo was awakened by music a little after 3:00 one morning. He followed the sound to the patio, where he found the maid and a young man embracing in the pool. Bottles of wine stood empty on the tiles. The air smelled of marijuana. The third maid cleaned better than the other two and could prepare simple dishes. But she also made long-distance calls to a village in Guatemala, which Ugo found in an old atlas in the library, the phone bill in one hand, the other tracing over the long indigenous names.

Then there was Paola. She was in her early thirties, not much younger than Ugo himself, and she had Felipe. In less than a week, under Bettina's direction, Paola cleaned, washed, or polished every object in the house. The furniture even smelled of fresh lemons again.

Ugo's mother did not remarry after his father's death. "Great wealth brings with it great responsibility," she told him. "You can't mix with just anyone."

Until Ugo was eight, he slept with his mother. They shared the big house with their two servants. Ugo liked it when Mrs. Norcross polished the furniture and it smelled of fresh lemons. Mr. Norcross drove the old car and kept it shiny. He also oversaw the gardeners who came once a week in the summer. From his room, Ugo watched the gardeners ride their tractor mowers over the grass until he could not see them in the distance.

Ugo went everywhere with his mother. Her hairdressers played games with him at the salon. He clung to her when she went to the bank. A serious man in a dark suit escorted them through the vault door, to the back, where they kept the safe deposit boxes. The muted light and the dark blue carpet made everything quiet. There were tiny rooms too that reminded him of confessionals. The man carried the safe deposit box inside one of the rooms and left. His mother locked the door before lifting the lid of the box on the table in front of her. Ugo stood next to her, his arm on the back of her chair.

He was allowed to play in the fitting area of the couturier at which his mother had stopped modeling and was now one of the biggest clients. It was there that he first saw a woman other than his mother undress. The louvered door to one of the fitting rooms was open. A broad-backed woman slipped out of a gown and handed it to an assistant. The woman stood in her underwear, looking at herself in the mirror. Then the assistant turned, saw Ugo looking, and shut the louvered door.

At home, his mother read to him while he drew pictures in bound sketchbooks that she ordered from Florence, using colored pencils made in Belgium. Ugo started school when he was six years old. His mother walked him to the headmaster's office on the first day of class. She adjusted his bow tie, tugged his jacket, kissed his forehead, and left. The other boys made fun of the lipstick mark on his forehead and nicknamed him "Romeo." The first week, he cried every day. But soon, he made friends. And though the boys still called him Romeo, they began to include him in their games. Two years later, when Ugo was in the third grade, his mother received a note from the headmaster observing that Ugo might get better grades if he paid attention to the teacher. The headmaster thought Ugo should be moved behind one of the better students.

Mayra Bonnet was the daughter of a prominent Cuban family who had owned three sugar mills and a distillery in Oriente Province, where they made a rum so strong that the bottle had a separate label warning of fire hazard. In 1961, when Castro expropriated the family's properties, they boarded a Pan Am jet to Miami. They lived off the interest on millions of dollars banked in New York, Geneva, and, it was rumored, a promissory note signed by the Vatican.

Mayra was slim and quiet. She had very white skin, black hair, and green eyes. With the unconditional approval of Ugo's mother, the headmaster ordered the teacher to move Ugo closer to the front, behind Mayra, who was a model student, in the hope that he would learn good study habits.

His heart jumped when he first saw Mayra up close, carefully guiding her pencil over the paper. He fell in love with the thinness of her wrist, the back of her neck, her ponytail.

When Ugo tried to get her attention, she complained to the teacher that he was distracting her. *The teacher warned him to be quiet. Mayra turned in her desk, looked at Ugo, and smiled.*

When he tried to sit near her during recess, she complained to Mrs. Griffith, who wore her hair in a beehive and whose only job at the school was to watch the children and sell them snow cones. "Little boys do not bother little girls," Mrs. Griffith told Ugo. Mayra laughed.

This was also about the time that Ugo broke his front tooth. It happened during afternoon recess. Two groups of boys played tug of war. Ugo joined in. Unaccustomed to physical exertion, he lost his footing and fell face-forward. His mouth would not stop bleeding, even after the school nurse arrived and applied a compress. "Oh dear," the headmaster said, when he saw Ugo's bloodied mouth.

The dentist fitted Ugo with a temporary cap over the broken tooth and promised his mother that he could have a permanent one when he was older. Though the temporary cap remedied the fearsome appearance of the jagged front tooth, it also felt as thick as a finger and smooth like varnished wood. And it throbbed.

Back in class the next day, Ugo rubbed the back of his hand against Mayra's sweater, just to touch something that belonged to her. The teacher could be talking about the longest river in the world or the capital of Mongolia, but Ugo was in the land of Mayra.

Two weeks later, he was finally alone with her. It happened during morning recess. Mayra walked in the girls' line, next to Ugo. She tugged on his elbow, and asked him if he wanted to sit with her. Ugo nodded, though he was unable to find his voice.

Mayra bought a cherry snow cone from Mrs. Griffith. Ugo did too. "Cherry is my favorite," she said. They sat on a bench under a large oak tree, where it was shady. He watched her take a small bite of the ice cone. When he did the same, using his front teeth, he felt a sharp pain, like a nail being hammered through his upper gums into his nose. Ugo cried out, dropped the snow cone, covered his mouth with his hands, and fell to the dusty ground.

Mrs. Griffith screamed. The headmaster arrived. Ugo's mother was called.

The dentist replaced the cap and warned Ugo not to use his front teeth for anything. "Bite with the side of your mouth," the dentist said, demonstrating with his own finger. But Ugo was not hungry. He was in love.

At home recovering, he thought about Mayra. He had seen his mother preen when she stood in front of the mirror trying on different necklaces. He had seen her brim with satisfaction when she opened the velvet-lined box on her dresser where she kept her rings. His mother had so many rings, she would not notice if he took one and gave it to Mayra.

That night, he ate dinner by himself in the upstairs dining room (a lukewarm soup, a truffle omelet, which he mostly picked at with the tines of his fork, pushing the little black flecks to one side). Ugo's mother was out having dinner and would not return until late. When he was finished eating, he folded his napkin and pushed himself away from the table. He went to his mother's bedroom, got the jewelry box, and opened it.

There were pearl, diamond, and emerald necklaces. There were necklaces made of stones Ugo had never seen. He held them around his neck and looked in the mirror. All were too big. He picked through the rings and found a small one with a round, red stone the color of cherry syrup. Mayra had said cherry was her favorite.

Ugo took the ring. He tore a sheet of drawing paper, selected a crimson pencil, and wrote, "Mayra," in block letters, many times, until he covered the sheet. He wrapped the ring in the paper and tied everything together with string he found in his mother's night table. It wasn't as pretty as the gifts he got at Christmas, but it would do. Then he hid the wrapped ring in his valise, a supple leather bag with Ugo's five initials in gold on the flap. The gift made a bump in the valise the size of a baseball. He pushed the valise under the bed and waited for Mrs. Norcross to come and tuck him in.

When Ugo returned to school the following day, his friends circled around him before class and asked him about his tooth. Did he ride in an ambulance? Did he get stitches? Did it hurt? He saw Mayra enter the classroom and slip her purse and books under her desk.

He sat in his place, behind her. And as the teacher called roll, her hand reached for the back of her neck and dropped a small piece of wide-ruled paper, folded in half. He picked up the paper from his desktop and opened it. On it was a smiley face that Mayra had drawn carefully. He was dizzy with excitement.

The teacher called out Ugo's name a second time, louder, before he answered, "Present." The teacher glared at him and moved down the list. Ugo's mind was fixed on Mayra's note. He thought of handing her the ring there, but that was too risky. The teacher would catch him, and he would be sent to the headmaster's office.

At recess, Mayra sat with some girls on the bench under the oak tree. Ugo sat at another bench nearby with two boys who were arguing about whether men would make it to the moon within the next three years. One boy said he expected the Russians to pull some stunt at the last minute, even if they had to crash-land and abandon one of their cosmonauts on the moon, just to say they got there first. "Your father's a commie working for Castro," the other boy said. Ugo sat holding a paper bag containing the wrapped ring, as if it were lunch, summoning the courage to walk across the yard and give it to Mayra. But the two boys got into a fight and wrestled on the ground, kicking up a cloud of dust. Mrs. Griffith pulled the boys up by their ears, blew her whistle, and signaled the end of recess. Ugo walked to class clutching the paper bag.

It wasn't until the last period of the day, while the teacher wrote the homework assignments on the board with his back to the room, that Ugo got his chance. He leaned forward and handed the bag to Mayra, making sure to keep it out of sight. She slipped it under her desk.

The bell rang and the teacher dismissed the class. Mayra took the paper bag and placed it on top of her books. Before she left, she turned, smiled, and made a little wave.

The next morning, Mayra ignored Ugo. If their eyes met, she looked away.

At lunchtime, Ugo was called to the headmaster's office, where besides the headmaster himself, he found his mother and a man he had never seen before.

The headmaster began by quoting Aristotle and Cicero, speaking about the duties of a good citizen, which he called civitas, *enunciating each syllable,* kee-wee-tahs, *he said, glancing at Ugo's mother for approbation, citing the school's commitment to inculcating* bonhomie *in the students. He spoke so much about the school that an uninformed observer would have assumed, quite reasonably, that the old man had gone into his sales pitch and that Ugo's mother and the other man (ceremoniously introduced by the headmaster as Señor Bonnet) were one of the many well-to-do parents who inspected the school before deciding whether to enroll their child.*

The headmaster spoke about Our Troubled Times, the vulgarity of it all, sanctioned as it is by the permissive vacuousness of psychologists and social workers with insipid the-o-ries, *he said, who, shall we be frank, have introduced into the stream of history the hissing water serpent of moral relativity and cultural equivalence, which, like an undetected cancer, is a malformed notion, a half thought, an idea so insidious that they have managed to replace* virtus *with fame and celebrity with notoriety, as if they were one and all the same. "Great for advertisers, but poison for the soul!" the headmaster said. He showed no signs of slowing down.*

Instead, he went back, all the way back, to the first "dysfunctional" family, he called them, to Cain's envy of Abel, to the moral miasma of Sodom and Gomorrah, to Paris snatching the beautiful Helen. "Damned hubris!" the headmaster said, tapping the top of his desk, pronouncing the foreign word so carefully that Ugo thought the old man would uncap the lovely gold and lacquer pen on his desk and write it out for them in Greek, as he liked to do on the blackboard when he spoke in class. "In short, persons lacking good citizenship," the headmaster said.

That would have been the perfect moment to conclude this little monologue, this bumper car ride through canonical myth, but instead of explaining the purpose of the meeting—"You're probably wondering why we have summoned you"—the headmaster digressed again, and Ugo felt as if he were strapped in a carnival ride, the one where the car spins on two axes at once and you lose all sense of up or down.

The headmaster's monologue spun past the humanists like Vittorino da Feltre, Leonardo Bruni d'Arezzo, and Petrus Paulus Vergerius, the old man savoring the names the way he sucked on cough drops. It took his mother, growing visibly impatient, to state telegraphically the purpose of their meeting, the raison d'être *of their* petite réunion, *which was a phrase she liked to use with her friends, as in—We must have another one of our* petites réunions—*but in the headmaster's office, the two words were heavy and thick and maybe a little sour, like eating the leftovers of Mrs. Norcross's Christmas Eve fruitcake on Epiphany.*

"The purpose of our petite réunion," *Ugo's mother said.* "Forgive me for interrupting you, Dr. Locasto." *The headmaster bowed.* "The purpose of our gathering here, Ugo," *she said,* "is to ask you one question: Why did you take my ring?"

Ugo looked at his mother, then at the floor, then out the window at the erasure of a cloud on the horizon. The grandfather clock in the corner ticked unchallenged.

"If I may say something," *Señor Bonnet said, his voice meek, as if he were embarrassed for breaking the silence.* "I was taken aback when Mayrita brought home such an extravagant gift from Master Ugo." *He talked directly to the boy. Although thin and neat in a dark, tailored suit, Señor Bonnet had none of Mayra's arresting beauty. He was pale, and his face was drawn, as if from sipping too many early-morning magnums of the old Dom.* "So I called the lady last night," *he said, one hand opening in the direction of Ugo's mother,* "surprised as I was to have found the telephone number in the phone book, grateful that you have such unique last names. And although we were not able to talk until late this morning, I explained the situation, and she quite graciously agreed to meet here."

Señor Bonnet had called her Mayrita, Ugo thought. Ma-hee-ree-tah, like the sound of wind blowing open an unhooked screen door to a single bright birdsong of a note, before the screen door slapped closed against the wood frame. Ma-hee-ree-tah.

"Why did you take my ring?" *his mother said, in six flat basso notes.*

"Young man," *the headmaster spoke,* "have you anything to say that might elucidate, at least adumbrate, this situation for us?"

Ugo's front tooth started to throb. The bell rang. For an instant, he felt relief as he thought the headmaster would call the meeting to a close. After all, classes were resuming and we must never be late for class. Didn't the headmaster say that when he caught you in the hall? But he remained silent. Everyone stared at Ugo.

I love her. Ugo thought he heard himself blurt out the words. I love her. I love her. I love her. I—

"My dear Señor Bonnet," the headmaster began again, "I do thank you for bringing this matter to our attention. Apparently, the child is under the influence of one of the darker muses, nowhere near the midpoint of his life and already well on his way down la via smarrita, if you get my drift. But we shall take it from here."

Señor Bonnet nodded to the headmaster. He said goodbye to Ugo's mother, who said she was so sorry, so je ne sais quoi.

To which Señor Bonnet raised his hand, as if to say "No hay de qué, my dear lady." At the narrow oak door, Señor Bonnet turned to look at Ugo and winked. Then he stepped out.

The headmaster ushered Ugo into the waiting room, "Much to discuss, yes?" and remained behind with his mother for another hour.

During the ride back to the house, Ugo's mother warned him not to tell anyone, not a soul, what he had done. He would be moved to the back of the class again, seeing as it was abundantly clear that his interests lay not in his school lessons but elsewhere. And he was not to talk to that girl. "I don't want any more trouble," she said. But the admonishments did not stop there.

"I am getting a lock for my room," his mother said. "It is difficult for me to accept the notion that I should have to lock myself in my own bedroom, in my own house, but there it is. And you will never step inside my room for anything. You will never go through my things, either. You will have your own things and I will have mine."

What his mother did not tell Ugo during the short ride was that she had negotiated with the headmaster the terms under which he would be allowed to remain at the school. He had been caught stealing. The headmaster knew about it.

"Dear lady, please," the headmaster had told her in his office behind closed doors. "It isn't as if I can feign ignorance and thus transmogrify myself into an accomplice."

But she managed to persuade him that the matter need not become officially one of theft. "The ring has been returned to its rightful owner, n'est-ce pas?" she said, holding up her hand. The ring with the cherry red stone was on her smallest finger. "If only we could look at this as a case of one preternaturally hormonal garçon taking too close an interest in a beautiful young girl. Not exactly a crime, is it? Of course not. Kind of cute, isn't it? After all, the girl, I have been told, is quite beautiful. If anything, we should celebrate his good taste, no doubt the result of having absorbed so much fine culture in these august halls," she said, turning in her chair as if she were only now taking in the art on the walls of the headmaster's office, mostly reproduction English hunting scenes. Ugo's mother knew how to play the game as well as the headmaster, who, frankly, preferred not to have to exercise his authority and expel the child when there were other, more fruitful ways to resolve the issue.

"The school could use an arts center," the headmaster said, "for the students to stage plays. The dramatic arts, while a base means to earn a living, when used judiciously in the pedagogical context, could be a salutary adjuvant to the traditional curriculum. A substantial contribution would go a long way to making the center a reality."

Ugo's mother agreed. And so numbers were discussed. The donation would be made anonymously, naturally, and the center named generically.

"I shall make note of it right away," the headmaster said, as they were concluding. He looked on his desk for his gold and lacquer pen. He patted the pockets of his jacket, like a smoker looking for his lighter. He opened the top drawer. "Oh, dear," he said. Finally, he settled on a disposable pen, one of those throwaways with the school name and coat of arms, and wrote a note to himself, frowning at the pen when he clicked the point out with his thumb.

At home, Ugo's mother instructed Mr. Norcross to furnish one of the bedrooms at the other end of the floor with whatever he thought a young *boy like Master Ugo would like. Meanwhile, Ugo would sleep in one of the other bedrooms that were reserved for guests.*

Mr. Norcross bought a modest bed, a dresser, and a desk, furnishings that Ugo's mother would have considered beneath her son's station, even (why not say it?) utilitarian or belonging to some other unpalatable cult, except she never entered his room. He never entered hers again. When Ugo's room was ready, Mr. Norcross moved his things in. Ugo's solitary life began in earnest.

Every day, Bettina arrived at Ugo's house in the late morning and stayed about two hours. She spent most of the weekends there, lying by the pool or sitting in the library talking to Ugo. Weekday nights, he sat alone in the library and read for hours, taking notes, if not copying entire passages. He used a beautiful gold and lacquer fountain pen that he kept in the center drawer of the desk. He wrote in the same leather-bound books his father had used. There were stacks of blank notebooks in the cabinets behind the desk. Bettina came over one Thursday afternoon, excited and out of breath.

"I just pledged a ridiculous amount of money to the museum of art," she said. "Now we'll be invited to all their special events and meet interesting people."

"But I know nothing about art."

"What about these paintings?"

"They've been there all my life. I wouldn't know if they are good or bad."

"Art is not about good or bad anymore. We're going to the cocktail tonight. Each first Thursday of the month, during the season, the museum holds a wine and jazz cocktail."

"Bettina, I don't like going anywhere."

"I love it when you use my name, even if you think you're going to have an argument with me."

"We're not arguing. And I'm not going."

But he did go. He agreed to accompany her because he felt a strange sensation in his chest, a minor oppression, like an invisible hand bearing down on the uppermost portion of his sternum, as if he had done something wrong and needed to make amends. Bettina had assumed the day-to-day management of the house. She had hired Paola, the gardeners, and the pool guy. She had called a telephone repairman to replace the black rotary phone with one that had a keypad and numbers that lit up so you could see them even when the room was dark. She had found a silversmith who reproduced the stolen utensils. She had the ancient Rolls-Royce repaired. And she hired a driving instructor. The instructor gave Ugo one lesson before he quit when Ugo refused to drive out the front gate to the street. Bettina had done so much for him already. In return, she had asked him to accompany her to the museum one night a month for a couple of hours. How could he refuse her?

The museum was more pleasant than he expected. The wine was unremarkable and served in plastic glasses, but after a few drinks, it became easy to swallow. In the corner of the large entrance hall was a jazz band. The trumpet and trombone were very loud in the mostly empty space and made conversation difficult. Bettina steered him from one group to another and introduced him as her "neighbor," her "gentleman-friend," and her "confidant."

"Why did you call me that?" Ugo said loud enough to be heard over the music.

"Because I tell you everything," she said before kissing him on the cheek.

The evening would have been a complete success had Ugo not committed a small faux pas as they toured one of the last galleries. By then, he had drunk three glasses of wine and his stomach was groaning with hunger. A middle-aged woman talked very loudly to the man next to her, as if she were lecturing a hall full of students, so no one but Ugo heard his stomach groan. The woman said, "Now *that* one I like." Or "Now *that* one I don't like." Ugo stayed close to the woman to avoid any embarrassment.

Then he saw a pile of wrapped candies in the corner of the gallery and walked over. On the wall above the candies was a card with the name of the artist and the title of the work. *Portrait of My Lover,* the card read. Ugo assumed that the card referred to the blank space on the wall next to it (there was a small smudge on the wall, about the size of a finger, that could have been the lover captioned on the card). When his stomach groaned again, he bent down, took a couple of candies, unwrapped them, and popped them in his mouth.

"Ohmygod!" a woman gasped.

"I think it's performance art," someone said.

It's stale, Ugo thought.

"Sir, sir," an old man in a guard's uniform stepped in front of Ugo. "You can't eat the art," the guard said, pointing at the pile of candy on the floor.

Bettina, who had drifted away for a few moments, returned. "What happened?"

"This man says I was eating the art," Ugo told her.

"This is definitely performance art," the same someone said.

Someone else shushed her.

"He didn't know," Bettina told the guard.

"I appreciate that, ma'am, but I'm going to have to report this," the old guard said before speaking into a tiny mouthpiece hidden under the lapel of his jacket. More guards arrived.

"Let's go," Bettina pulled on Ugo's arm.

"Just a minute there, lady," the old guard put his hand on her forearm. She shook it off. "This gentleman has just committed an act of unprovoked vandalism."

"Now, wait a second—" Bettina started to say.

"What's happening here?" It was the museum president, a thin woman in her sixties, wearing a black dress and a pearl necklace. The crowd let her through.

The old guard explained what happened.

Bettina introduced Ugo.

"Of course, I've heard all about you," the museum president took both his hands in hers. "And Bettina says that you're going to be serving on our board."

"I am?"

"We're very excited," the president said.

The guard cleared his throat.

"Oh," the president said to the guard, "I'm sure we have more candy in the back."

"But he ate two of them!" the guard cried out.

"Maybe the artist won't mind if the work is two candies short," Ugo said, trying to be helpful. "We could ask him."

"The artist is dead, sir," the guard said.

"If the artist can see us, wherever he is," the museum president said, looking at the ceiling, "he must find this very funny." She laughed and turned to the crowd.

Scattered applause. Ugo smiled.

"I'm still hungry," Ugo told Bettina when the applause died down.

Soon after Ugo was ejected from his mother's room, she started to travel for a few weeks at a time. The door to her bedroom was closed and locked. His mother sent unsigned postcards addressed to Mrs. Norcross. Ugo kept the postcards and placed them in the box with his father's logbook and the photograph. He used the old atlas in the library to mark the places where she went.

When Ugo was thirteen, his mother took a trip around the world on a yacht owned by the richest cattle rancher in Brazil. A year later, she returned with gifts for everyone. Mrs. Norcross received a leather purse from Argentina and a silver rosary from Italy. Mr. Norcross received fine cloths from England and two cases of champagne. Ugo got a miniature bullfighting ring from Spain, a pair of ebony bookends from Ethiopia, a collection of poems by Rimbaud in French, The Divine Comedy, illustrated and abridged for "young ladies and gentlemen" in modern Italian, and a samurai sword from Japan. Ugo's mother announced that she was tired of traveling and would be staying home for a while. She needed to rest, she said.

Instead of rest and quiet, the house throbbed with mambos, rumbas, and cha-chas playing from the stereo console that Mr. Norcross wheeled out to the patio. Handsome young men, and women his mother's age, danced and drank around the pool, wearing only their bathing suits, sometimes less.

One day, as Ugo walked toward the dining room, a woman called out, "Oh, there's the son." The woman wore sunglasses and a one-piece black bathing suit. She called Ugo over. When the music started again, she took his hand and made him dance with her. She smelled of chlorine and cigarettes. Ugo kept his head down and looked at her feet, so as not to step on them. Each time he tried to leave, the woman pulled him closer. "That's no way to treat a lady," she said. "Do you have a little girlfriend?"

"For chrissakes, he could be your son," one of the men cried out.

"I'll let you know," the woman yelled over the music, "that in some cultures, more advanced ones, if you ask me, it is the mother, or, if not the mother, then the aunt, who initiates a young man."

"Don't let his mother catch you practicing anthropology without a license," another man said.

"She's too busy with Nico," the woman said, and immediately put both her hands over Ugo's ears. "You didn't hear that."

There were other parties. New people replaced the old ones. Bossa nova and samba played from the console stereo. Each morning, Mr. Norcross brought the stereo inside and cleaned the polished cherry wood cover. A fine white powder seemed recently to crosshatch all the flat surfaces near the pool. Ugo saw a young man inhale the powder through a straw off a glass table. He spied a woman in the library with one of the framed Matisse etchings on her lap. The woman ran the tip of her finger over the glass before she rubbed it against her gums. After the woman left to join the others, Ugo took the etching and did the same with the remaining specks. His mouth was numb for hours, and he bit his tongue twice.

On another day, Ugo walked past the door of the music room and saw a naked young man crouching, flipping through the LPs. The man looked barely twenty. He was thin and muscular. Two outspread wings were tattooed on his lower back, and his buttocks were very white. Then Ugo's mother walked across the room, also naked. She knelt down and embraced the man from behind. Ugo left as quietly as he could.

· · ·

From the museum, Bettina drove Ugo to Le Bec Fin, a small, very exclusive restaurant on South Beach with a view of the channel and the large cargo ships that left the port late at night. On their way to the beach, she thought a car was following them. But before she made the final turn into the restaurant parking lot, the car disappeared.

At the restaurant, Ugo ordered two bottles of wine and drank most of it. When the check arrived, he had trouble reading it. He took out his wallet, put a bill down, and covered everything by turning the check face down over the bill. The waiter collected the check and bill, bowed slightly, and left.

Ugo could barely follow what Bettina was saying. The sound of clinking glasses and utensils seemed to grow louder.

"Excuse me, sir," the waiter returned. "There must be some mistake." He showed Ugo the bill and the check, a blur of letters on a rectangle that appeared to undulate, as if it were underwater. Then the ceiling lights flew past Ugo, and he heard a thump, which was the sound his head made when it struck the edge of the table before he slipped out of his chair and fell to the floor.

Ugo did not remember the rest of the night, not the argument between Bettina and the waiter, who thought Ugo had pretended to faint to avoid paying the check, not the part where two busboys walked him to Bettina's waiting car.

Nor did he remember how she helped him into his house (it's a good thing Paola was a light sleeper and came to the door as soon as Bettina rang the bell because she could not find Ugo's house keys), and the two of them, Paola and Bettina, each grabbed one of Ugo's arms, walked him to his bedroom, and laid him on the bed as Bettina said, "Thank you, Paola," and Paola said, "*De nada, señora,*" and "Call me if you need anything else."

"I think we will be fine," Bettina said, before she closed the bedroom door and locked it.

Bettina opened the balcony doors and took a deep breath. The breeze smelled of the sea beyond the barrier islands.

She loosened Ugo's tie and pulled it off before unbuttoning his collar. Then she sat him upright, his chin against his chest, to remove his coat. She took off his shirt too and laid him down again, his head snapping back against the pillow, his mouth lying open. She undressed him to his underwear.

Ugo mumbled something.

"What did you say?" Bettina whispered close to his ear. He snored softly.

Should she? Why not finish what she started? She pulled on the elastic waistband of his boxer shorts. She slipped her hand under his lower back and lifted as much as she could to slip off the shorts.

Ugo lay motionless. He looked like a boy—hairless, ribs showing, hipbones pronounced.

She turned off the lights, undressed, and lay next to him. She found his hand and held it. But she was tired and must have fallen asleep right away because when she opened her eyes it was morning and she had let go of his hand.

When Ugo was fifteen, he made friends with a girl in his class named Ana María. She was a little heavy and not very pretty, but she was friendly and outgoing. She dressed modestly, even carelessly, in baggy, simple clothes that looked as if she had slept in them. A month into the school year, they ate lunch together every day in the cafeteria. By November, they talked on the phone until late at night. The homeroom teacher reprimanded them for talking in class. "Would you lovebirds please stop your twittering so we can get on with the business at hand?" she said. Everyone laughed.

Boys who had never talked to Ugo before punched him in the arm and winked. "Did you do it?" they asked.

Ugo knew what "it" was after exploring the library at home, which included translations of classic Indian texts on lovemaking and Tang Dynasty medical books on sexuality, as well as Hippocrates, Galen, and Vesalius. Ugo had read Plato on abhorring women, Catullus on sweet-talking them, and Aristotle's Metaphysics, which quoted Parmenides, who claimed that desire was the beginning of everything.

He knew that human beings engaged in complex mating rituals that varied in different cultures and times, which in the case of Ana María and Ugo, included the exchange of handwritten notes during Geometry class. How do you divide a right angle? Let me count the ways.

It was the early seventies. Miami was going through one of its construction booms and Ana María's father was making millions. His picture appeared frequently in the papers.

Ugo's mother called Ana María and her family nouveaux. She said, "Girls like that are interested in one thing only." She meant money, but Ugo thought she meant sex and blushed. His mother prohibited him from seeing Ana María outside school, lest he mix with the wrong people. They did not see each other through Christmas vacations. The absence, instead of diluting the relationship, only strengthened it.

When classes resumed, Ana María drove to school in a new convertible sports car. A few times, she and Ugo skipped class to park on the causeway and listen to music. She gave Ugo his first kiss. They might have gone further except for the daylight outside, the stick shift between them, and the fact that Ugo had to return to school before Norcross arrived to collect him.

One afternoon, Ugo asked her if they could meet behind her house late that night. "Just like Romeo and Juliet," she said, which was what they were reading in English class.

Ugo set the alarm for 2:00 in the morning, but he didn't need it. At 2:15, he sneaked out of his bedroom and got his bicycle out of the garage without waking the Norcrosses. Then he set off for Ana María's house, having memorized the route on a street map.

The roads were dark. The moon was a crescent and hung suspended over the horizon. The city lights washed the sky clean of stars. Ana María's house had a wall around it and a curving concrete driveway that ended at a wide garage door. There was a broad lawn too. Beyond that was uncleared land that turned into mangrove before it met the bay.

Ugo hid his bicycle in the bushes, climbed over the wall, and ran across the yard, following her detailed instructions on where they would meet. Behind the house was the pool and the patio. Beyond that was the tiled path she said would lead him to the gazebo and the artificial pond.

"Hey!" Ana María whispered. She sat on coral rocks that rimmed the pond. Everything was dark except for the spotlights on the main house in the distance, which seemed to shine directly at them. "Everyone's asleep," she said. "We're safe." She wore a white tee shirt, shorts, and sandals. Ugo stepped carefully on the rocks. "The pond's not deep, but don't fall in because I'm not going to rescue you." she said, giggling.

Ugo sat next to her. She took his hand and leaned against him. The coral felt hard and sharp. Then she kissed him. "Like this," she said, slipping her tongue past his lips.

She stood, stepped in front of him, and placed her arms around his neck. She sat down on his lap. A sharp point in the coral rocks beneath him jabbed his thighs and made him wince. They kissed some more, but the pain worsened. When he tried to relieve it by lifting himself off the rock with Ana María on top of him, he lost his balance and she fell back.

Ugo heard a splash and the sound of hollow metal being struck by something blunt.

"Ana María?" he called out, trying to keep his voice low. The pond did not reflect any light.

He stood rubbing the back of his thighs. A breeze blew and made the palm trees hiss. Something moved nearby.

"Annie?" Ugo walked around the pond, still rubbing his thighs. A few yards away, the overgrowth of broad leaves and vines appeared black and impenetrable. As he approached it, the air smelled of rotted fruit and sulfur. A branch snapped.

"Aah-neeh?" Ugo said, almost in a whisper. Something was moving away from him. The sound came from deep inside the overgrowth. He tried to see, but there were too many leaves, thick, with skin like rubber. Behind him, from the house, he thought he heard the drawn-out squeak of a door hinge. Without thinking, Ugo parted the vines and stepped into the overgrowth.

The sky disappeared. A little light from the main house seeped through a break in the leaves behind him. More noise. There was something out there, maybe someone had heard them and was coming to investigate. He took a few more steps, careful to avoid tripping over the roots, until he was in complete darkness. The vines grew thicker the deeper he went. Far above him, the leaves rustled, but the breeze did not reach him.

Another branch snapped.

"Ana María, please!"

He moved in the direction of where he heard the branch snap. And as he did, the vines embraced him and the leaves felt waxy against his face. The roots wrapped loosely around his legs. He lifted his feet to keep from tripping and took one step every few seconds, feeling with the tips of his shoes before placing his weight on the spongy ground. The vines were so thick that when he leaned his shoulder into them, they pushed him back.

She must have become scared and run, he thought. Or maybe she was hiding, waiting until it was safe to come out. No one would find them hidden this deep in the vines. It was black. Except for the ground pressing against his shoes, he had no sense of up or down. There was only the smell of the mangrove nearby and the sound of the open bay beyond that.

He would wait. He would stand still, close his eyes, and think of nothing except being here. It was good, sometimes, just to be, to close your eyes, let the world continue without you. As a child, he spent hours hiding in the unused rooms of the house.

"You have inherited your father's reclusive genes," his mother told him one summer when he was six and the Norcrosses found him only after searching the entire house. "And look where those genes took him."

To seek solace in the middle of the ocean, Ugo thought. To escape you.

"Your father thought only of himself," his mother said. "Il était un égoïst sans pareil. First him, then him, and once again him," she said. "People like him take so much from the world and give so little in return. They are cursed to live in solitude and die of loneliness."

But it was peaceful to be alone, Ugo thought. Even more, to remove oneself from one's thoughts, like stepping into a world where nothing happened.

He thrust his fists through the leaves and extended his arms until he stood like a diver ready to jump. He did not think about what he did next. He did not think about anything. He leaned forward and let go. The vines held him suspended above the ground.

Ugo waited for the sound of another branch snapping, but there was only the white noise of insects. The black around him was so thick and unmoving that it seemed as if he were floating in it. When he closed his eyes, phosphorescent crystals darted each time he tried to look at them.

He dreamt. He saw an endless expanse of lawn. The noon sun. Whiteness. And out of the whiteness, a figure began to emerge, but before he could recognize the figure, he opened his eyes.

The moon shone above him, a wispy gray arc within a sphere of light that made everything luminous. The vines and the ground were the color of ashes. How long had he been there? Ana María was likely back in her room asleep.

Ugo untangled himself and felt his way out of the overgrowth, back to the pond. He ran through the yard, climbed back over the wall, and found his bicycle in the bushes. He pedaled home so fast that he almost lost control.

The following day, Ana María did not go to school, nor the day after that. On the third day, the teacher announced to the class that she had been found dead. "An accident," she said. A card addressed to her parents was passed around for everyone to sign. Ugo signed too. By end of the day, a rumor started circulating that her body had been found in the artificial pond behind her house. The police had evidence of foul play. They found footprints near the body that they believed were made by the murderer. The footprints went around the pond, into the overgrowth, then out to the wall at the edge of the property. A smudge marked the place where the police thought the perpetrator had jumped over the wall.

Late the next morning, the sound of the gardeners' tractors mowing the grass below the bedroom balcony woke Ugo. He felt as if someone had stabbed him through the eyes. Each time he turned his head, the room banked. He inched his way to the edge of the bed, sat up, waited for the room to settle down again, then stood.

Had he undressed himself? When he looked up, he heaved. He ran to the bathroom and kneeled in front of the toilet bowl. Waves of nausea flowed through him until he spit out a thick yellowish liquid so sour it caused him to retch again, even though nothing else came up. The tap water tasted sweet when he washed his mouth in the sink.

The gardeners finished mowing and the tractors rode away. Ugo heard three quiet knocks on his bedroom door.

"Paola?" he called out. Bettina walked in. Ugo dashed behind the bathroom door but kept his head in view. The room was spinning less than before, but it was hot and he was sweating.

"I've already seen you naked," Bettina said. When she took a step toward Ugo, he shut the bathroom door and locked it.

"Hey," she said, her mouth pressed against the door. "Listen to me: Did I ever tell you that—"

The first shot pierced the French doors that led to the balcony and shattered one of the panes. Ugo tried to unlock the bathroom door, but the old, defective lock would not release.

Another shot hit the dresser mirror. A third shot thumped against the wall. A fourth smashed through the bathroom door and whizzed past Ugo's right ear, causing him to jump into the bathtub and slide the glass doors shut. It was quiet for a few seconds.

"Bettina?" Ugo called out.

"I'm all right," she said.

A fifth shot hit another window, followed by two more shots in quick succession. Something heavy fell to the floor.

Downstairs in the yard, a man screamed, "You bitch! Come out here!"

Ugo climbed out of the tub and ran with all his strength against the bathroom door, tearing the 110-year-old hinges off the wood frame, landing face-first. He crawled toward the bed and crouched behind it. He spit out the cap on his front tooth and wiped the blood off his mouth with the back of his forearm.

Bettina lay on the floor in front of the open balcony doors.

"I know you're screwing that faggot!" The man sounded drunk.

"Bettina," Ugo said just loud enough so only she could hear him, "we should call the police. Did you hear me?" His gum was bleeding. It tasted coppery.

He crawled toward her. The back of her head was red and bright.

A dark stain on the carpet beneath her spread slowly. The room smelled of the freshly cut grass and blood.

Ugo covered his face with his hands and sat on the floor, his back against the bed. Only when the man started screaming again did he crouch to the floor and crawl toward the balcony doors until he got close enough to peek.

Ugo recognized Bud Alvarez from the pictures Bettina had shown him. Alvarez stood in the yard below the balcony wearing a dark suit and an open-collar white shirt. He had his back to Ugo. Suddenly he turned around, aimed the gun at him, and squeezed the trigger three times. Ugo ducked out of sight, but he heard the *click-click-click*.

"Come out here, you faggot! And bring my wife with you!"

"*¡Dios mío! ¿Señor, qué sucede?*" Paola was on the other side of the bedroom door, which had shut and locked.

"Paola," Ugo said, "call the police. *La policía.*"

"No, not the police, *señor.*"

"Yes, Paola. The police. Now!"

Ugo peeked again. Bud Alvarez was still there, staring up at the sky, his eyes wide open, holding the gun by his side.

The police arrived a few minutes later. Ugo sat next to Bettina's body. He placed his hand on her back and let it rest there. His eyes filled with tears until the balcony doors, the room, and the morning light blurred. The bedroom door burst open. A dark unfocused figure stood in the doorway.

"Police. Are you armed?" the officer asked Ugo. The question, as ludicrous as it was, made Ugo feel a little less naked.

The gardener found Ana María's body early the next morning. He lifted it out of the artificial pond and laid it on the grass. He had a severe speech impediment, which made questioning difficult when the police arrived. Though they found nothing linking the gardener directly to the murder, the circumstantial evidence made him the prime suspect. He was found not competent to stand trial and committed to a mental hospital, where he died of a heart attack eight years later.

Ugo finished prep school in Switzerland. He enrolled in a small liberal arts college in Vermont and majored in classics. He never graduated. His senior year, his mother became ill with cancer, and he returned home.

She died months later, when he was twenty-two years old. He inherited the house, the rococo furniture, a library of leather-bound books in five modern languages and two dead ones, an eclectic collection of nineteenth-century paintings by obscure French artists, and an ancient Rolls-Royce. And the money, of course.

The information filed by the state against Bud Alvarez included one count of first-degree murder for the death of his former wife and three counts of attempted murder for pointing the gun at Ugo and squeezing the trigger three times. Bud Alvarez pled to a lesser charge and was sentenced to life in prison. He also lost a civil trial for wrongful death. The jury awarded Bettina's estate punitive damages in excess of seventeen billion dollars, a sum 250 times greater than his entire worth.

For almost two years, Ugo kept to himself, turning down invitations to dinners and cocktails. On weekdays, before the sun set, he liked to watch Felipe play outside the house with his schoolmates. When the boys got too loud, Paola ran out to quiet them.

Ugo enrolled Felipe in a private school and paid his tuition.

"Felipe has something to tell you, Don Ugo," Paola said one afternoon, standing in the hall outside the library. "Go ahead." She nudged her son inside.

"*Gracias, señor,*" Felipe said. "Thank you, very much."

"You're welcome, Felipe." Ugo held out his hand. Felipe shook it and stepped back into Paola's arms.

Ugo went to the dentist and had a new cap placed over his tooth. Otherwise, his days began and ended the same way. On those rare nights when he felt restless, he reread portions of *L'education sentimentale* or *La vita nuova* and saved Catullus for the end, which he could recite in Latin with his eyes closed. *Da mi basia mille, deinde centum.* The woman he imagined had Madame Arnoux's black hair,

Beatrice's green eyes, and Lesbia's husky voice. *Dein mille altera, dein secunda centum.* Some nights he imagined Bettina loosening her long black hair over her shoulders. *Deinde usque altera mille, deinde centum.* Other nights, it was Ana María who appeared uninvited, still fifteen, her arms across her chest, her skin wet and cold. She stood for a moment. Then she ran across the room and disappeared.

3.

La verdad es que Neruda dice que es bien largo el olvido,
pero mi opinión personal es que es bien largo el recuerdo.
—Alfredo Bryce Echenique

Twenty-two months after Bettina died, Ugo attends the first wine and jazz cocktail of the season at the museum. He looks forward to the company of others, the small talk, the music, even the art. His life feels settled again, like stepping on land after being out at sea.

Inside the museum, people are kind to him. They are well-mannered enough not to brood on tragedy, so they talk of other things as soon as it is appropriate.

The museum president comes by several times, makes sure his glass is full, and walks him through the first gallery. "Here's an exciting new find," she says, pointing to an unmade bed in the center of the floor.

Not long after he arrives, unused to so much activity around him, Ugo begins to feel tired. He takes his leave and walks out into the humid night.

The driver he hired by the hour insists on playing music. Ugo wants silence, but the driver is excited and punches buttons on the console through the entire trip, skipping from piece to piece.

At home, he pays the driver. "Guy, you can call me anytime, OK?" the driver says, handing Ugo his business card. HAPPY TIMES, reads the name of the limo company.

Paola and Felipe are in their apartment over the garage. Ugo thinks about sitting in the library for a while, but whatever contentment he felt earlier has come apart.

He climbs the stairs to his room and undresses. He lies on the bed and turns off the light. The air glows like the night sky over a distant city. He thinks about taking a sleeping pill and reaches over to the night table when he sees her.

She stands in the corner with her arms held tight across her chest. Ugo is not afraid. She's done this before. She never speaks, never looks at him. Each time, she stays a little longer. But her skin is wet and she is shivering. Then she starts to run across the room, as she does every time, as she has done for years on nights made restless by the hum of an unwelcome memory.

Ugo lies in bed for a long time, trying hard to think of nothing.

He stands and opens the balcony door, the only one that works after the other one was shot.

The shrimper boats are out. Spotlights hang face-down off the sides of the boats. He hears the rumble of their engines and the men on the boats singing. A breeze rises and the palm leaves rustle around him, drowning out the engines and the men.

Ugo stands on the balcony and breathes deeply. He looks at the lights on the bay and the shrimper boats.

He read somewhere that the spotlights hanging off the boats attract the shrimp to the surface. Shrimp confuse the lights for a full moon. Once on the surface, they are scooped up with nets.

Shrimp are stupid, Ugo thinks. *"Ils sont cons,"* he says.

Con is a word his mother would not have liked to hear him use, so he says it again. *"Con."* And again. *"Con."* Louder. *"Con. Con. Con."*

He says it so many times that he can hear it even after he stops.

Nothing

It was past midnight and Lincoln Road was crowded with tourists and locals. Near the corner of Meridian Avenue was a café where you could have tapas and wine. They served stronger drinks too, but they were expensive, even for South Beach. Outside on the sidewalk, an umbrella with the name of the café stamped on it spread over every table. All the tables were occupied and extra chairs had to be brought from the back to accommodate all the customers.

More people arrived. The wait for an outside table grew to over an hour, and latecomers had to settle for a place indoors.

Inside the café, the stucco walls were painted burnt orange. Un-framed canvases made by local artists hung on the walls—rectilinear abstracts, sensuous still lifes, and portraits of women reclining like *majas*, except for the homicidal look in their eyes. The air was thick with the warm smell of cigars. The smoke rose until it disappeared between the blades of the fans. Painted on the ceiling was the windmill scene from *Don Quixote*. If you asked about the artist, the manager himself, Estefan Roig, came to your table and explained that the painter slept on the beach, kept everything he owned in a small backpack, drank only Chianti, and told everyone that he was the reincarnation of Michelangelo.

Also in the back, two young men strummed nouveau flamenco on their guitars. They wore red bandannas wrapped around their heads and blousy white shirts. The guitarists took turns performing solos that Roig suspected were recorded. Speakers fixed to the walls and above the entrance carried the music out to the street.

Even with five waiters and two bartenders, service lagged and customers complained. One woman was served a daiquiri instead of a mojito, another received limoncello when she had ordered a *caipirinha*, and a strongly built bald man who looked to be in his forties, with a goatee, big arms, and an accent, was incensed about getting a snifter of brandy after he had ordered cognac. He sat at one of the larger tables outside, near the entrance. Next to him was a young blonde with vaguely European features wearing a tight knit top.

"I told him," the bald man pointed at the waiter, a wiry Cuban named Manolo, standing next to Roig. The speakers were almost directly overhead and the music was loud. Roig leaned forward so that he could hear the man. "I even showed him the menu here," the bald man said, "so your man would not make a mistake." He wore a huge gold watch and a gold bracelet. The blonde said something to him in a language Roig did not recognize. She was in her early twenties, at most. She wore an expensive gold necklace and a diamond watch.

"I know this trick," the bald man said, ignoring the blonde. "You bring me brandy and charge me for cognac. I call the police." He started to push his chair back from the table. Roig apologized and offered them a round of drinks on the house.

Manolo walked behind Roig to the bar.

"Charlie, *dos coñacs*, for table twenty-seven," Roig called out to one of the bartenders. Then he turned to Manolo, put his hand on his shoulder, and said, "I know you are doing the best you can under the circumstances."

"But these are impossible circumstances!" Manolo said.

Roig removed his hand. "It is what it is, and we have to make do."
He turned his back on Manolo and spoke to the bartender again.
Charlie was twenty-five and claimed to have graduated from phar-
macy school in Cuba. Roig was grooming him to become assistant
manager.

The guitarists finished their set. They had played for less than
fifteen minutes. Lately, their breaks had stretched from thirty to
forty-five minutes. Roig would have a talk with them.

When the drinks were ready, Roig placed them on a tray with a
bowl of olives and another bowl of peanuts. He carried everything
outside to the table with the bald man and the blonde and he served
them.

"How do I know this is cognac?" the bald man said, pointing at the
glass.

"It is the cognac you ordered," Roig said. "I served it myself."

The man picked up the snifter and swirled it. He raised the glass
to his face, breathed deeply, and took a drink. "Good," he said,
smacking his lips.

The blonde leaned over to kiss him. Then they both turned to Roig
and brought their hands together, as if they were applauding.

Roig loved his job. Restaurants and cafés were all he had known since
he left his parents' apartment almost thirty years before. His father
had been a jeweler. After school and all day Saturday, Roig helped
him at the workshop, sweeping and cleaning mostly, watching him
mount diamonds on rings and pendants. His father did not believe
in free time. "Every minute of our lives on earth is borrowed," he
told Roig. He frowned on idle conversation, card games, and vacations. "Frivolities," he called them, using the Catalan word. Still, he
did not object when Roig's mother took him and his brother, Emilio,
to her cousin's farm for three weeks during summer vacation.

The first time they went, Roig was twelve years old. He woke
before the sun rose to work in the kitchen grinding coffee beans in a

big iron mill bolted to the wall. After breakfast, he pumped drinking water from the well. "Look at the shoulders he is developing," his mother said. Emilio, in turn, slept late and read paperback novels all day. Roig also played with his cousin, Elena, who was a year older than he. She taught him to care for the horses.

For five years, Roig's mother took her sons to the farm. When Roig was fourteen, Elena let him ride behind her. When he was fifteen, he kissed her, and her lips were so soft that he had to touch them with his fingers because they did not feel like skin. The rest of the year, they wrote long letters to each other.

His last time at the farm, the kisses led to long walks in the afternoons to places where no one could find them. Elena did not discover she was pregnant until Roig was back home. The two families met and decided that marriage was the only honorable solution, so Roig fled.

He took a train to Madrid and worked as a waiter, changing jobs each time he learned that someone had come around looking for him. When he turned twenty-one, he flew to Venezuela and worked his way from waiter to maître d'hôtel and finally to manager of one of the most fashionable restaurants in the Chacao district of Caracas. He stayed there twenty-four years and married the daughter of an Italian immigrant, a woman with black eyes and curly black hair. They divorced two years later when he discovered that she was pregnant by another man.

He did not hear from his family again until his last year in Caracas, when he received a letter from Emilio. His father had died of lung cancer, and his mother had died years later of a stroke. There was also a photograph of his brother sitting with his own family. Emilio was in the center, next to his wife. He had lost most of his hair. She had a plain face and veiny hands. Standing behind them were two young men. On the back of the picture, his brother had written, *Here we are—me, Elena, Estefan, and Mauricio. We named the eldest one after his uncle.*

For weeks, Roig thought about writing back. Several times, he started to compose the letter in his head. Then Chávez came to power, Cuban military advisers arrived from Havana, and the army replaced many civilian teachers. Roig followed the owner of the restaurant and moved to Miami.

Roig left the bald man and the blonde to stand at the café entrance, from where he welcomed customers and walked them to their tables. He also watched people walk on Lincoln Road, past the café. He could distinguish the Europeans from the South Americans and the Americans. The French traveled in pairs, usually couples, burnt from too much sun. The English came in small groups of pale and rowdy young men. The South Americans spoke softly and examined the menu carefully. The locals were easy to spot too. They left the best tips. Then there were what he called the very locals, the beautiful young people who lived on South Beach. They were tanned and fit and wore few clothes. They always had their cell phones out, talking into them or thumbing messages. There were others too—performers, pamphleteers, a man who sang the 1958 hit "Volaré" in different keys, a juggler, and a one-armed crazy.

Roig called him El Loco, the Crazy One. Each time the police took him away, he would be gone for a few weeks. When he returned he was a different person, smiling at everyone, rattling a bottle of prescription pills at Roig as if it were a party trick. But then the pills ran out and he harassed the customers again. He had a real name, which a police officer told Roig was Caine. "Just like the actor," the cop said, laughing. But to Roig, he was El Loco. He was short, with sunbeaten dark skin. His hair was blond and matted. His eyes were a feline green. When someone gave him money, he danced a jig and bowed low, his one arm across his chest and the stump of his other arm, amputated below the elbow, jutting out behind him. If people waved him off, however, he screamed and chased them, swinging his stump over his head like a club. There were other crazies on Lincoln

Road—like the woman who dressed in brown garbage bags wrapped with twine and marched past the café arguing vehemently with herself—but they never bothered anyone.

One night, a few months before, while Roig was occupied in the back behind the bar, El Loco walked to a sidewalk table at which two fashionably dressed older women were seated. He took the unoccupied chair across from them, drank wine from their glasses, and ate their olives and cheese.

Manolo told Roig, who called the police before he ran outside. The women were standing, clutching their purses, while Caine picked at the olives with his fingers. Roig escorted the women inside the café. Two officers arrived on bicycles.

"Get out of the chair!" one of the officers yelled. Caine lifted a glass of wine and toasted them. The officers tackled him out of the chair and knocked the bottle and the glass to the sidewalk. The red wine seeped into the limestone.

After that, Charlie kept a bat hidden behind the bar. Caine disappeared for a while, but now, with business picking up, he had returned.

From the café entrance, Roig watched El Loco at the corner across the street, holding out his hand and begging for money. Two women stopped. One reached into her purse and dropped a coin into his palm. The other woman held a video camera and taped him dancing.

Roig walked to the back of the café. Every stool at the bar was taken. Other people stood with their drinks. Charlie poured vodka into a shaker, put the lid on it, and shook it so vigorously that several people turned to look at him.

"How are we doing?" Roig asked Charlie as he poured the frothy drink into a martini glass on the bar.

"We cleared two thousand."

"I told you it would be a good night."

"It's about time."

"When you get to be my age, you can tell."

"You talk as if you were an old man."

Manolo interrupted them with an order for six drinks. Charlie started to work on the order.

"How is table twenty-seven doing?" Roig asked Manolo about the bald man.

"They are only two sitting at a table for four. We have a full house. And they have been nursing the same drinks for almost an hour. Complimentary drinks, I should add."

"Let me worry about that. You worry about your tip."

"Europeans don't tip," Manolo said and went back outside.

"What's the matter with him?" Charlie said.

"He's old."

"Lately it's gotten worse."

"Lately he's gotten older."

Charlie prepared another order of drinks. Roig served himself a glass of soda water.

"Don Estefan!" A customer who was a regular waved at Roig with both hands from the other end of the bar. His name was Richard, but he called himself Ricardo and spoke Spanish. In the eighties and nineties, he had lived in Managua and married a Nicaraguan woman. He carried a picture of his young boys in his wallet. One looked mestizo, the other had lighter skin. He never told Roig what he did in Managua.

"My friend." Roig forced a smile.

"Looks busy tonight. I'm glad," Ricardo responded in Spanish. He put his cigarette out in an ashtray.

"Why don't I order you a couple of tapas? You shouldn't drink on an empty stomach."

"Better not. I'm on the South Beach diet—vodka and cigarettes. To busy nights and lots of money." Ricardo raised his glass. Roig raised an empty hand wrapped around an imaginary glass.

"I've never seen you drink," Ricardo said. "How can you run a bar and not drink?"

"That is the only way you can run a bar. I work sixteen hours a day, seven days a week. My father had no patience for *haraganes*."

"Must be tough on your family."

"You know I have no family."

"Have I shown you the picture of my boys?"

Roig nodded.

"I must bore the hell out of a lot of people, but I'm proud of them."

Roig knew that Ricardo had not seen his children in five years. Since their mother remarried, she had kept them from having any contact with him.

"Don't you feel alone, though, without a family of your own?" Ricardo said.

"I am happy to have this," Roig said, opening his arms.

"Don't give me that crap," Ricardo said in English. "This is your work, your daily bread, *hombre*. It is a good place, but a man needs more." He slurred the last words. "Man does not live by bread alone," he said, looking at his glass and drinking from it. "You should find yourself a beautiful young girl," he said in Spanish.

"What would a young girl, beautiful or not, have to do with a man my age? Besides, I prefer having them as customers. Then if something is wrong, all I have to do is serve them a round of drinks on the house and everything is all right again."

Roig felt someone tapping on his shoulder and was grateful for the interruption. It was the bald man asking him for the men's room. He walked him to the door. When he returned, Ricardo was busy talking to a man sitting next to him. Let drunkards comfort each other, he thought.

Roig stepped behind the bar and found a cigarette butt in his glass of soda water. He emptied the glass into the sink. The water fizzed like acid. Lying on a shelf over the sink was the bat Charlie kept hidden.

Who the hell was Ricardo to talk? Roig thought. He wouldn't recognize his sons if they walked into the café and sat next to him. What gave him the right to dispense advice? Of course Roig could have done a few things differently, but he harbored no illusions. He had failed as a son and failed as a husband. And if Estefan was really his son, as he suspected after examining for hours the picture Emilio had sent him, then he had failed as a father as well. Life offered no second chances. Why did he listen to Ricardo anyway? Talking to him always put him in a foul mood.

One of the guitarists walked in front of the bar. Roig caught his attention and tapped his wristwatch. The guitarist smiled, called his partner, and they sat down to begin another set.

Roig didn't want anything else. He had the café and that was enough. He arrived early in the morning to receive the deliveries and opened the front doors at noon. The café owner, a silver-haired man in his seventies, came by every weekday around 1:00 to go over the numbers. After the owner left, the café was quiet until sundown. Then people started to come in and Roig was busy until closing time. He usually went home at 3:00, when the surrounding streets were quiet, except for an occasional motorcycle or a car playing hip-hop so loud that the windows buzzed. It was a short walk to his apartment, and he was grateful for the solitude. On some mornings, the city was so still that when he opened the window, he could hear the ocean.

Manolo ran to the bar. "Chief, we've got problems," he said. "It's El Loco. He's molesting a customer."

Roig ran out from behind the bar. Charlie followed behind him with the baseball bat.

They found Caine sitting next to the blonde, pinning her against the wall. Two men at the next table stood ready to confront him. Roig motioned for them to sit down, but they remained standing. He told Manolo to call the police.

"You like my girlie-friend?" El Loco said. He raised his stump and placed it across the blonde's arm when the baseball bat slammed the table and sent the drinks into the air. People screamed. Caine ducked under the table. The blonde jumped out of her chair and ran into the crowd.

The music came over the speakers so loud there was feedback, a frenzied strumming of chords that made everything vibrate.

Charlie struggled with the bald man for the bat. The bald man pushed Charlie away. He pushed Roig too. The manager fell to the pavement and scraped the palms of his hands.

Caine looked out from under the table. The bald man swung again and almost hit him on the head. He raised the bat for a third swing. An arm holding an open straight razor sprang from under the table and slashed the bald man on the leg, tearing his pants. Caine leaped out and slashed the bald man on the arm and across his cheek.

The bald man dropped the bat, fell to his knees, and covered his face with his hands. Before anyone could react, Caine pushed through the crowd and ran down the street. Only Charlie ran after him.

Someone must have disconnected the speakers because the feedback stopped and the guitars sounded faint and ineffective.

The police arrived, so did the paramedics. They treated the bald man and put him on a gurney and into the back of their truck. The blonde was sobbing.

Roig gave a statement to a police officer, who later handed him a card with a number written on it where he could call to find out about the case.

"What do you think will happen?" Roig asked the officer.

"You want the truth?" the officer said. "If we find him, we'll take him in. But he'll get out again. Life goes on."

Manolo brought a mop and a bucket of water to wash the sidewalk. Charlie returned panting. When Roig looked at him, he shrugged his shoulders.

People at the surrounding tables asked for their checks and soon there was no one left outside and a new crowd arrived to take their place. Roig fired the two guitarists, paid them off, and played CDs instead.

The café remained busy until closing. The staff stayed behind and retold the story, acting out the different parts, until Roig said enough and told everyone to go home.

Charlie helped him count the money and put it in the safe. Half an hour later, they turned off the lights and locked the doors.

"Wait," Roig said. "How about if we go somewhere for a drink?"

"Since when do you drink? Anyway, we have all the drinks we want in the café."

"Not there. And I don't want to go home. Not yet."

"Because of what happened tonight?"

"Maybe. I don't know."

If he went home, he would start to think, and he did not want to do that. Leave the philosophizing to the likes of Ricardo. Roig had the owner to keep happy, customers to please, and the employees to manage.

"Lead the way, then," Charlie said.

There was a small bar two blocks away that stayed open until sunrise. It belonged to another Spaniard, named Juan Carlos, an *isleño* from one of the Canary Islands. Roig had met him during the slow months and stopped by sometimes after closing the café.

"*Hombre*, how are you?" Juan Carlos called out. He came around the bar to shake Roig's hand and saw that they were scraped badly.

"What happened?"

"A long story," Roig said.

"At our age, all our stories are long."

Roig introduced Charlie.

"What would you like?"

Roig told him. Charlie ordered the same. Juan Carlos went behind the bar and talked.

Roig pretended to listen, but his mind started to think about Emilio again, even though he promised himself that he wouldn't. You let yourself think and soon you start to imagine what could have been, when the only real thing is the present. It is the only thing that counts.

Juan Carlos filled three small cordial glasses with chilled dry sherry. He placed the glasses on the bar in front of them. The cold sherry made the glasses cloud.

There is the now, Roig thought, and there is only the now. Nothing else matters.

Juan Carlos placed two small plates with green olives and slices of Manchego cheese cut into triangles and a shot glass full of toothpicks on the bar.

Roig would forget. He would burn Emilio's letter and the photograph and throw out everything else that he did not use. He would reduce himself to the present, accept who he had become without thinking about how he had arrived there.

He reached for the glass of sherry. It felt cold and thick. The bar lights shone on the rim and through the base. He raised it.

"¡*Salud!*" Juan Carlos said, raising his own glass.

The Sleepless Nights
of Humberto Castaño

Humberto Castaño couldn't sleep. When he closed his eyes, he saw his daughter talking to boys, flirting with them, kissing them, having sex with them. Humberto saw Dodie letting boys into the house after school, while he and his wife were still at work. He imagined her lying in bed, the boys on top of her, backs arched and shiny with sweat.

When Dodie turned sixteen, he and his wife threw a big party and let Dodie invite her friends. There were a few girls, but mostly there were the boys, drunk on hormones.

Dodie was beautiful. One Sunday afternoon on Lincoln Road, an agent gave Humberto her card and said that he should let his daughter model. Last year, Dodie was first runner-up for Miss Calle Ocho. She would have won if the winner's father were not a bigwig in the Little Havana Kiwanis Club. Everybody said so.

A few weeks ago, after dinner, Humberto picked up the phone and heard a boy crying. His wife told him that the boy was Dodie's friend from school. He'd been calling her cell phone and getting voice mail. His wife felt sorry for the boy so she put him through to Dodie.

Our daughter's a heartbreaker, his wife said.

The next morning, Humberto asked Dodie about the boy, but she cut him short.

He's just a person, she said.

On weekends, Humberto took Dodie and her girlfriends to the mall. He pretended to drive away. Instead, he parked nearby and ran back. Inside the mall, he followed them from a distance, jumping behind columns, running into stores, mingling with the crowds of shoppers to avoid being seen. In the movie theater, he sat in the back and hid his face behind a family-sized tub of popcorn. He was convinced that Dodie and her friends had agreed on a time and place where they would meet boys, go to the house of one of the less vigilant parents, and have sex. Thoughts like that kept Humberto awake.

In the middle of the night, he would slip out of bed and walk on the tips of his toes down the hall to stand outside Dodie's bedroom, listening for any sound of movement, voices, bedsprings. Once, he heard a woman's voice, opened the door, and caught Dodie talking on her cell phone. Humberto took the phone back to his bedroom, turned on the light, and scrolled down the list of calls received. His wife recognized the name on the screen. It was the crying boy.

As punishment, Humberto prohibited Dodie from meeting her friends, talking on the phone, and going online. For a week, she came home from school, completed her assignments, ate with them, and went to bed early. Humberto was happy.

A week later, when Dodie could go out again, she told her parents that she was meeting her girlfriends on South Beach to see a movie. She said one of the moms would be there to chaperone. Humberto dialed the woman's phone number. Each time, he got an answering machine. He wanted to follow Dodie and the girls, but he could not break his promise to take his wife out for dinner on their anniversary.

When Humberto and his wife returned home, a squad car was parked outside the house. A police officer sat on the living room sofa. He introduced himself and told them that their daughter was upstairs with his partner, a woman officer who had kids about the same age as Dodie.

She's in good hands, the police officer said.

Humberto's wife ran up the stairs.

The police officer told Humberto what had happened. Dodie called 911 after her date jumped into the ocean and drowned.

Humberto recognized the name of the crying boy.

The sequence of events is unclear, the officer said, but around 8:3o, Dodie and the boy were at the end of the pier on South Beach when he climbed the rail and screamed that he was going to jump. People tried to talk him out of it. The water's full of boulders there, stuff left over from when they made the jetty. The boy jumped anyway and broke his skull. Good thing your kid's taking it so well, the officer said.

Humberto did not look in on his daughter until after the police left. He found his wife rearranging the pillows behind Dodie, who was sitting up in bed, pointing the remote control at the TV.

From then on, Dodie withdrew to her room. Some weekends, her girlfriends slept over. They watched movies and listened to music. The house vibrated with the sound of hip-hop, but Humberto didn't complain.

When Dodie left to attend college, he and his wife drove her to the airport. They were silent on the way back home.

That night, Humberto slipped out of bed and walked on the tips of his toes to Dodie's bedroom, as he had done many times before. He did not turn on the light. He knew where everything was. He felt his way to the bed and brought her pillow to his face. He took a slow, deep breath and held it. Dodie's scent was not there. He lay on the bare mattress and buried his face in the pillow. He almost did not hear his wife.

The ceiling light blinded him for a moment. His wife stood in the doorway, looking very small. Her eyes were closed tight and her hands were cupped over her nose and mouth. It was a long time before she said anything.

Bay at Night

After dinner, the doctor and his wife walked through the colonial city to the boulevard that skirts the bay. Everything was dark because of the blackout. The only light came from the moon, passing cars, and the lanterns off the sides of the shrimper boats. The fort at the entrance to the bay, usually lit for the tourists, cut a black square against the night. Couples sat and kissed on the low concrete benches next to the boulevard. Boys and young women offered their wares and services to the tourists. The doctor's wife found an empty bench and sat. He stood behind her. The moon lit a strip of water from the horizon to the rocks below them. Each time the water crashed against the rocks, the sidewalk trembled under their feet.

"Are you scared?" she asked him.

"Let's not talk about that tonight," he said. "It doesn't matter, does it?"

A car with one headlight stopped next to the curb. Loud dance music played through the open windows. Two men and two girls stepped out and sat on a bench a few yards away. The headlights of a passing car caught them. One of the men was thin and young and looked like a local. The other was middle-aged and looked Slavic—short blond hair, beefy. The girls were bony, in their teens.

The doctor's wife closed her eyes and raised a hand to her face.

"Want to take a cab back to the hotel?" the doctor said.

"I'm OK."

"It's not too late, you know."

"I thought you didn't want to talk about it. Besides, we talked about it in Miami. It was too late from the start."

"I hate it when you talk like that. You didn't used to," he said.

"It hasn't been easy for you, has it?"

"That's not what I meant."

The music sped up. The girls pulled the beefy man off the bench and danced with him. One girl raised her arm for the man to duck under before she passed him to the other girl, faster and faster, until the man was unsteady on his feet.

The music stopped and started again, but the beefy man stood panting. His shirt was dark with sweat. He tried to bow and stumbled. The girls applauded. Then they helped him sit.

"I love you for what you've done," the doctor's wife said.

"I've done nothing. You haven't let me."

"But you didn't need to come here. I know what it would mean to you, to your reputation, if word got back."

"Maybe we shouldn't talk so loud."

"OK, so we won't talk about that either," she said.

"I didn't say that."

"But you're right. What's left to talk about? I've made up my mind."

She stood and walked a few steps, away from the car and the music.

The doctor looked at the bay. Below him, a small boat with two men stopped near the rocks. One man held a net and the other shined a lantern over the dark water. The lantern illuminated the men's faces, chests, and arms, and spread dabs of yellow on the surface of the bay.

"Do you have a light?" It was one of the girls. She smelled of flowers and sweat. The doctor dug into his pant pocket and found a box of matches from the hotel restaurant. When he gave it to her, his fingers grazed the palm of her hand. It felt callused and rough.

"Thank you, sir," the girl said in English. She tossed the matches to the thin man, who looked at the doctor and shook the box over his head.

"Guess what I have," the doctor's wife said, walking toward him, holding a bottle.

"I don't know."

"I don't either. The boy said it was rum, but I think it's just moonshine with food coloring. Three dollars. Can you believe it?"

"That's not worth three pesos."

"What's three dollars to us?"

"A lot. To them."

"Then I did something good for someone. What gives you the right to have a monopoly on good works? Here, you first."

His wife removed the wad of paper that served as a cork and held the bottle in front of his face.

"If you won't, I will," she said. He watched her drink from the bottle. When she finished, she stuck out her tongue. "That's the worst thing I've ever tasted."

He took the bottle and drank, forcing himself to swallow.

"Do you want one of those girls?" his wife said. "They're not ugly. A little skinny maybe."

"Why are you talking to me like that?"

"Just thinking, that's all."

"You're being cruel."

"Drink some more." She drank quickly. "It's hard for a man to live without a woman," she said. "A woman can live alone, but a man always needs a woman."

"I've tried to be a good husband."

"I have few complaints."

"I've done everything you've asked," he said.

"No, we did mostly what you wanted."

"For the love of Christ, tell me what you want me to do and I'll do it."

"Promise me that you'll have children. Promise me that you'll find yourself a young wife, someone smart and pretty, who can paint watercolors or play the piano and host charming dinner parties that you can invite your colleagues to, someone who can bear you smart and pretty children with perfect table manners. Promise me."

"I don't want to think about that."

"I never gave you children."

"We didn't want any, remember?"

"You didn't want them. Your research. That's what you said."

"And you agreed."

"And I'm sorry I did that. I'm more sorry than you can ever know. And now it's too late." She raised the bottle to her mouth but did not drink. "Promise me. Just say it. What's so difficult about that? Señorita?" his wife stood and called in the direction of the two girls, who were helping the beefy man to the car. "Señorita," she called again.

The thin man ran to her.

"How much for the girls?" she asked him.

"I don't want any girl," the doctor said, taking her arm.

"I am sorry, but I do not understand," the thin man said. "They are occupied, as you can see."

"Excuse us," the doctor told the thin man. "There is some mistake."

"How much?" she said.

"They are very good tour guides," the thin man said. "We are here every night. Tomorrow." He smiled before returning to the car. The girls and the beefy man waited inside.

"We'll find another girl," she said. "They seem to be everywhere."

The car started and drove off, taking the music with it.

It was quiet, except for the water. The moon was higher in the sky, smaller. Then the streetlights came on and lit the city and the fort.

"Now they ruined it. It was so lovely before," she said.

"You must be tired."

His wife swung the bottle into the air and waited to hear it smash on the rocks.

The doctor walked to the curb to wave down a cab. When one stopped, he went back to help his wife.

"You didn't promise," she said.

"How can I promise you something like that?"

"Say it. That's all I'm asking. Just say the words."

"If that's what you want."

She nodded.

"I promise," he said, offering his arm to her.

"I'm OK," she said. "I'll be fine."

A Natural History of Love

1. GIRL LOSES BOY

Less than twenty-four hours after Rolly broke up with me, my best friend, Gloria, calls to tell me that she saw him and Lizette Caballero at Cocowalk leaving the movies, holding hands and kissing all the way down the escalator to the parking garage.

"Like I care," I tell her.

Rolly and I were just friends. We talked on the phone every night. He took me to the movies twice, and we skipped school once. Several times, we made out in his car, but I never let it go further than that, not much anyway. And though we came close, we never actually did it. We dated for twenty days, twenty-one hours, and forty-seven minutes, if you start counting from the moment he first said hello to me in the school library.

"Are you sure it was Rolly?" I ask Gloria, feeling stupid as I say the words.

"Of course, Silvia. They walked right past me. Rolly *and* Lizette."

I hang up. I don't want to hear it. If Gloria calls back, I'll tell her the call was dropped. Happens all the time. Cell phone service sucks. And, anyway, I need to think.

Then I get this pain deep in my chest, tears well up in my eyes, my mother walks into my room, and my cell phone chirps, all at once.

"What happened?" Gloria says when she calls back.

I don't want to talk to anyone right now, but at least the phone protects me from having to talk to my mother. If she sees me crying, she'll give me advice. She can't help it. Giving advice is like a disease with her.

I start to answer Gloria, but I can't speak. More tears. I toss the phone on the bed.

"Hello? Hello?" I can hear Gloria's voice, even after I cover my face with the bed sheet.

My mother sits on the bed next to me, puts her arm across my shoulders, and pulls me close to her. Just what I need. I bring the bed sheet up to my ears. Maybe she'll get the message and go away. She kisses the back of my head, takes the phone, and tells Gloria that I can't talk right now. "OK, honey?" my mother tells her. The phone goes clunk when she puts it on the night table.

My mother says, "I know how you feel."

I think, No way she knows how I feel. My parents met in high school and married in college. She's forty-one. I'm not even seventeen, and already I've failed twice.

"Tomorrow you'll forget all about him," my mother says.

I think, Who told you this has anything to do with a guy?

My mother says, "There are other fish in the ocean." She adds, "No hay mal que por bien no venga."[1]

I think, This is supposed to make me feel better?

She wants to kiss my face, but I'm holding the bed sheet tightly, so she kisses the back of my head again. She stands. I hear my bedroom door close. I exhale.

---

1. My mother knows a bunch of stupid sayings in both English and Spanish. One of the benefits of growing up in a bilingual home is that you get to be lectured in two languages.

2. THE LAW OF SUPPLY AND DEMAND

I listen for a few minutes to make sure my mother's gone. There's a chance that she'll come back and officially tuck me in for the night.[2] My cell phone chirps again and again. I've known Gloria to call twenty times, back to back. She lets the phone ring until it goes to voice mail, hangs up, and calls again. Over and over. I want to turn off the phone, but what if Rolly calls?

In my bathroom, I wet a small towel with warm water and wash my face. The blueberry acne mask falls off my face in dried chunks. It reminds me of something I saw on TV earlier tonight—a house going down the side of a cliff in an L.A. mudslide. The whole house came down in one piece as the ground collapsed below it.

Thirteen missed calls, the phone screen says. Every time it starts to chirp, I can't help looking at the screen to make sure it's not Rolly.

When I'm done washing my face, I return to my bedroom. Eighteen missed calls, the phone screen says. I think, Listening to music would clear my mind. The Sonic Skulls are good, so's Ten Monkeys on My Back, but what I want right now is something to relax me, make me forget about Rolly, Gloria, my mother, everything.

I pick the Tin Hearts, put the volume on low, mute the phone, and turn off the lights. If Rolly calls, I'll still be able to read the screen. By the third track of the Tin Hearts, I'm feeling better. The chest pain is gone. I try to forget that it's Saturday night, not even 10:00, and that I'm home lying in bed, like a dork, trying to think of nothing.

I don't think about Gloria at the mall watching a movie with Teri O'Donnell and Francesca Gutierrez, probably that new one we were

---

2. My mother feels that tucking me in and giving me a good-night kiss on the forehead is her maternal duty. This feeling no doubt stems from a deep-rooted sense of guilt due to the fact that her mother, my grandmother, Nana, raised me from birth until she died when I was thirteen. During that time, my mother billed mega-hours and made partner at her firm and now is totally dissatisfied with her career. She's making up for it by infantilizing me, trying to experience what she missed. I should put an end to this practice, but I don't want to cut her off cold turkey. There's no telling what kind of trauma doing that would cause her.

talking about seeing together. Earlier this week, Gloria invited me to go with them, but I told them that I planned to go with my boyfriend, and my insides trembled a little after I'd said the word "boyfriend." That was three days ago, Wednesday.

Rolly was not my boyfriend. Not officially. We just ended up together. It felt comfortable to hang out with him, like wearing cotton pajama pants and an old tee shirt to bed. I felt like Rolly and I were *supposed* to be together. My mother says that she was fated to marry my dad. OK, where can I get some of this fate?

3. THE BREAKUP

Yesterday, after school, I asked Rolly if we were still on for last night. He nodded. He can be very serious sometimes, moody even, so I didn't think anything of it. The plan was he'd pick me up at 7:30 and we'd drive around, think of something to do. I was going to suggest the movie. That way I could tell Gloria that I'd seen it and tease her with the ending. But at 7:35, after I'd finished spraying the last of my mother's Chanel, he called me to break up.

I couldn't believe he was serious. Only a few days before, Rolly had held my hand between classes. We'd even parked on the causeway and kissed.

Several times last night, I thought about calling him back. Mr. Núñez, our AP Economics teacher, says that the law of supply and demand determines the price of goods and services. "You got too much, you pay less. You got too little, you pay more. Is scientific." So I didn't call Rolly. I decided to make myself scarce. That alone should make him want me back.

4. HOW TO NOT THINK ABOUT WHAT YOU'RE THINKING ABOUT

This morning, I woke early and surprised my mother by going with her to do errands. As a reward, she bought me a linen blouse and a pair of prewashed jeans with holes torn at the knees from a little store off Bird Avenue. Nothing is free in life, so I had to put up with hearing her complain about paying so much for a pair of jeans that she would have consigned to the trash can. My mother likes to use words like "consign."

All day, I was sure Rolly would call me to apologize and make it up to me. Everything took on the sheen of expectation. An immense goodness enveloped the world. At home, I worked on tearing the holes on the jeans some more. I sat on the chaise longue in my father's study, my cell phone next to me, tearing at the holes with my fingers until I got them the right size.

After a quiet dinner with my parents, I went to my room and watched TV.

That's when Gloria called me to say that she'd seen Rolly *and* Lizette Caballero.

But I forgot. I'm trying not to think about him. I tell myself not to think about Rolly. *Do not think about him at all.* I cover my head with the pillow and hum and listen to the way my voice sounds when it has nowhere to go.

Don't think about anything, I think.

I look for something else to play. The problem with music is that there's a limit to the number of times you can listen to "Throbbin' Like an Aneurysm," even if it's the coolest song you've ever heard.

I play some Ninja Babies from the only CD they ever made before they broke up.

There's a happy phrase—they broke up—like Rolly and me.

5. THE ONLY THING GUYS THINK ABOUT

I turn off the lights, close my eyes, and try to concentrate on the lyrics. Instead, I replay everything Rolly said when he called me yesterday. It wasn't a long conversation. Two minutes, two seconds, by the timer on my phone.

"Hello?"

"Hey. What are you doing?" Rolly said, enunciating every syllable. Rolly's a stickler for good language. He always says "well" when other people say "good." He never says "anxious" when he means "eager." He thinks people who use "home" and "house" interchangeably have tufts of dryer lint instead of brains.

"I'm ready," I said. "You coming over?"

"That's part of why I'm calling. I'm not going to be able to pick you up."

I paused.

"OK," I said. "You wanna meet somewhere?"

He paused.

"Not exactly," he said. "I can't really go out tonight. I can't see you."

I think I hear someone giggling.

"Who's there?"

"No one," Rolly said earnestly, but I don't think about it until much later, long after we've hung up and I'm replaying the conversation in my head.

"What's the problem?" I said. "We made plans."

"I just prefer if we don't go out tonight."

"Oh," I said, feeling the beginnings of anger stir inside me. So what am I supposed to do now? I thought.

And maybe Rolly interpreted my one-word answer—"Oh"—as a sign of disinterest, because his voice changed. I don't mean that it broke in the crackly way characteristic of pubescent boys. I mean that he went from sounding unsure, almost embarrassed, about canceling our plans at the last minute, to speaking with something like gravitas.

"I really don't want to see you this weekend," he said.

I let a second or two follow that one. It wasn't deliberate on my part. My father says that silence in a conversation can be more eloquent than words. But in this case, I didn't know what to say. Then I remembered finals were two weeks away. And that Rolly, due to some less than stellar marks on recent quizzes, needed a near perfect score to keep his average. Of course he couldn't go out with me, I thought. He was panicking about finals. He had to study. How selfish of me to think only about myself.

"If it's something I can help you with—" I said.

"I *don't* want to see you anymore," he said louder. "OK?"

Two letters that are not an abbreviation for anything and can mean so many different things, depending on the tone of your voice. I'd never heard him talk like that before. The dumping experience was a new one for both of us, whether you looked at it from his perspective, as the party doing the dumping, or mine, as the party being dumped.

"Are you, like, breaking up with me?" I said.

"Yes. I am breaking up with you," he said, pronouncing each word as if English were a foreign language.

A more experienced person would have thrown a light-voiced "OK" right back at him. Or maybe a single cutting "Fine." She would have hung up and called another boyfriend or girlfriend and gone out anyway. The entire evening, she would have enjoyed herself and not discharged a single synapse in her brain for Rolly. A more sophisticated person would have dropped the phone into her tiny, elegant purse. She would have looked in the mirror, refreshed her lipstick, and gone out by herself. I imagined her wearing a little black dress and heels, adjusting the front of her dress over cleavage that I do not have, pulling down the skirt over hips that I do not have either. If only I looked more like that, I thought, I'd grab my little purse, walk out to my car, and leave.

"But why?" I asked Rolly, hitting myself in the thigh for sounding so whiny. Now it was his turn to pause for a second or two.

"It's because you don't put out," he said. "OK? You tease me, but you don't deliver."

I'm thinking that I should really be mad at this point. I should tell him to go—

"It's all about sex with you," I said, trying my best to sound indignant.

"Yeah," he said, as calm as the surface of a man-made lake.

I knew he'd hung up because the screen on my cell phone lit the side of my face.

6. THE PROBLEM WITH SUNDAYS

I turn on the light. It takes a couple of seconds before I can read the digital clock on my night table. Almost 1:00 A.M. Gloria, Teri, and Francesca are probably home by now. I start to call Gloria when my thumb punches Rolly's number instead.

My heart races. You cannot break up with me, I think, if I do not want to break up with you.

The phone rings four times. His voice mail comes on. *Hey, you know the drill.*

I press Redial. Four rings. Voice mail. *Hey, you know—*

I hang up and press Redial. This time it goes straight to voice mail.

So Rolly's turned off his phone. I keep calling. Every time I hear his voice, I press Redial. I almost leave a message once, but the words never migrate to my lips from wherever it is words are born.

Sunday is my least favorite day because there's all this free time to think. I wake at 9:00 and stay in bed another half hour. Mrs. Eden, my AP English teacher, gave me a five-page paper to turn in on the last day of class. She assigned essay topics to the top five students in the class for extra credit. The first four topics were "courage," "honesty," "fairness," and "loyalty." Really drab stuff. Then came my turn. "And Silvia," Mrs. Eden said, "gets to write about love," which she pronounced dragging the word out, stretching the vowel, ending on a soft vee, which caused the boys in the class to whoop and howl. Some of the guys made smooching sounds, craning their necks, kissing the air.

Gloria, Teri, and Francesca later said that I'd gotten the best assignment. Gloria joked about all the research I would have to do. She made quotation marks in the air with her fingers every time she said the word "research."

We were leaving the classroom when Mariella Poza, class president for two years in a row, favorite to be crowned homecoming queen next year, came up to me and said, "You wanna trade?"

Mariella's a very tall and thin brunette. Some people think she is the most beautiful girl in the school, so beautiful that they call her Mari Poza, a play on the diminutive form of her name, which sounds like "butterfly" in Spanish. She has a near perfect grade-point average and drives a little red Mercedes sports car that she got for her sixteenth birthday. Her father's a plastic surgeon. He's the one who owns the two-story imitation Italian Renaissance palazzo on Brickell with the Venus de Milo fountain out front. His patients fly in on their own private jets from places like Caracas and Mexico City. He's operated on almost all the *telenovela* stars. The day Mariella first drove her car to school she caused a commotion. People gathered in the parking lot to look at the car, until Sister Anne came out and shooed them away. I was there, too, and made my way to Mariella, whom I had never met, and told her that she had a nice car and I hoped she enjoyed it. And I meant it. I'm not envious. But Mariella looked through me, like I didn't exist, and turned to talk to one of the football players, who was standing next to her and using words like "horsepower" and "torque," relishing the sound of his own voice. Now in Mrs. Eden's class, Mariella was tapping my shoulder, smiling like we were buddies.

"I said, do you want to trade?" she said. The topic she got was "honesty."

"No way," I said.

Her smile disappeared. "Fine," she said. "*Cómetelo,*" which literally means "eat it" but more accurately translates as "shove it." She turned and left.

"*Ay*, she's so rude" and "*Qué puta*," Gloria and Francesca said at once. "*Pooh*-tah times two!" Teri said.

I left the classroom that day thinking that I had the coolest assignment in the world. But that was early last week, before Rolly called me on Friday to break up and Gloria called me yesterday to tell me she'd seen Rolly with Lizette. Since Rolly's broken up with me, I am not so sure it's a good idea for me to write about love. Maybe I should have exchanged papers with Mariella and written about honesty, a no-brainer if ever there was one.

How do you write an essay about love, anyway? Do you write about the stuff you've experienced firsthand? If so, mine would be a very short paper, no more than a few lines:

Guy and girl meet. Guy and girl laugh, kiss; do everything but have sex. Guy dumps girl because they don't have sex. Bottom line: if you want love, have sex.

Mrs. Eden says a good essay must state a conclusion. It almost doesn't matter what the conclusion is, she says, so long as every sentence in the essay supports it. She says it helps to say something extraordinary, something that will catch the attention of the reader.

Bottom line, revised: if you want lots of love, have lots of sex.

Well, why not? If Montaigne could write about B.O. and Swift could write about eating babies, why can't I write about bartering sex in exchange for love?

Bottom line, revised again: the more people you have sex with, the more people will love you.

Because my parents would kill me, that's why I can't write that. They wouldn't get mad. They wouldn't nag. They'd just kill me.

7. A LIST OF EVERYTHING I HATED ABOUT ROLLY,
COMPILED WITH THE LAUDABLE PURPOSE OF
SNIPPING HIM OUT OF MY LIFE

✂ Each time Rolly and I were alone, he slipped his hand in
my bra.

Whenever I have a problem that I want to solve or at least understand, I make a list. Making a list helps me, even when the list con-
tains seemingly random and unrelated thoughts.[3] My father says that
by making lists you give your mind and, specifically, your unconscious a way of associating unrelated ideas and feelings, reconciling
what is seemingly unreconcilable. If you figure out the association,
or if you let your mind or unconscious figure it out for you, you can
discover some pretty interesting stuff about yourself. That's what my
father says, anyway.

At first, I felt self-conscious making lists, like everything I wrote
had to have some weight, like it had to matter. One morning, as I was
driving to school, I noticed the sunlight flickering through the leaves
on the tree branches that arched over the street. I'd seen that before,
of course, many, many times. I usually take the same route. It isn't
the shortest or the fastest. It is the prettiest way to go. But that morning, it was like I was seeing the sunlight for the first time. So I wrote
about it. Nothing flowery, just the facts—the name of the avenue, how
fast I was driving, a description of the trees, the time of the year, how
the sunlight flickered as a result of the motion of the leaves and my
trajectory below them.

Then I did some research on the Net. I learned what the trees are

---

3. Proof that my mother and I couldn't be more different lies in the fact that she abhors
lists, is totally allergic to them. Her grocery shopping is a cappella, resulting in un-
countable containers of iodized salt, canned soup to survive a thermonuclear war, fruit
punch to fill a lake, and toilet paper to stretch from here to one of Jupiter's moons.

called, when the city planted them, that they pollinate in October. On another Web page, I learned that flickering sunlight can cause seizures in some epileptics. I also learned that happiness can be caused by little things, like driving under an arch of leafy tree branches. But I had kinda discovered that for myself.

✗ Rolly detested all kinds of music (not just rap or hip-hop, which I could understand, but everything melodic, rhythmic, atonal, or otherwise), so we spent a lot of our time sitting next to each other in silence.

I showed Mrs. Eden the list I made about the flickering sunlight. She held the notebook in her hands. I had never before noticed the way her watchband sank into her flesh, the jewelry she wore, the dullness of the gold, the cheap blanched stones, how round her face was and how doughy her neck. She said I should write some more about my experiences, only the next time I should try to capture the essence of the experience, not only the facts. "The essence," she said, "is always more than the sum of all the facts. It's the holy grail of artists."

I've never thought of myself as an artist.

✗ Rolly wore button-down oxford shirts in white or blue, chinos, boxer shorts, argyle socks, and Bass Weejuns. The shirts and chinos were laundered and pressed. Sometimes he looked like a cardboard display for a boys' clothing store. Even his tee shirts had creases. He kept antiseptic wipes in the glove compartment of his car. He used at least three or four wipes after pumping gas. Then he sniffed his hands. The smell reminded me of my gynecologist.

Anyway, "facts are so numerous," Mrs. Eden said, "that you can never make a complete inventory." And even if you could fill a thousand pages about one incident—driving under the arched trees on a cool morning and watching the sunlight flicker through the leaves— a list would not help the reader experience it, which is what reading is all about. "To capture the essence," she said, "you need only a few well-chosen words." I should read some good poetry, she said, writing down the names of some poets and poems, the way a doctor scribbles a prescription. "Read a couple of these and we'll talk about them the next time," she said.

A few of the poets I recognized because Mrs. Eden hyperventilates about them in class. I wish I liked poetry, but I don't. Most poetry is nothing more than showing off—*The Jerry Springer Show* in truncated sentences and unconventional punctuation, arranged to look nice on the printed page. Take the poem that some English guy wrote to an urn. I looked it up: an urn is a pitcher, a vessel, a big flowerpot. You gotta be into some weird stuff to write a poem for a flowerpot. Now there's someone who deserves to be on *Springer.*

✕ Rolly hated TV. He didn't have one in his room.

You can never list everything there is to know about someone, even someone as bound to routine as Rolly. The point is to identify the most important elements of whatever it is you're describing or the most important qualities of the person you're trying to describe.

✕ Rolly's favorite word was "banal," which he used to describe everything in the known world and which he pronounced like the word "canal" as said by a foppish English character actor in a 1940s black-and-white B movie.

Lists are not a cure-all, but they do lend a certain degree of order to the world, like a tidy room: The bed is made. The shoes have been put away.

✕ If you said "white," Rolly said "black." If you liked something, he hated it. He argued about everything, took it to "its logical conclusion."[4]

So I made a list of reasons why I shouldn't give Rolly the time of day, even if he came back begging me to let him be my tampon. Writing the list made me feel better. I would snip him out of my life.

Finals were coming up. Then summer. And who knows, like my dorky mother says, there are other fish in the ocean.

8. A DIFFERENT KIND OF LIST

Not everything was bad about Rolly, though—

♡ I loved the way he drew the number nine. He'd start in the middle and make the head first, looping over clockwise to complete the tail.

♡ I loved our talks after school, not the philosophical ones, the others. The ones when he drove us to the causeway and parked on the beach to watch the sailboats and the parasails. There's a breeze coming off the bay so you could open the windows and kiss to the sound of the water lapping over the rocks.

We talked about our favorite writers—Haruki Murakami for me, any *manga* for him, so long as it had a bizarre title, like *Psycho Briefcase Emperors*. We talked about our favorite foods—sushi for me, pizza and cold leftover Chinese fried rice for him. Our favorite music— techno and deep house when I'm up, New Age and Baroque string

---

4. Brother Richard, our Religion teacher, sent Rolly to the principal's office last month when he ridiculed the idea of God. "Knock, knock," Rolly said, getting up in the middle of class and opening the door to the hallway. "See? No one there."

quartets when I'm down. Silence for him. "There's too much noise in the world as it is," he said, turning off the car CD player less than a second after I had turned it on. OK, that was annoying from the start.

♡ I loved our first kiss.

We had finished doing our homework in the library. That's where we started hanging out together. It was almost 5:00. I didn't want to drive home then because of the rush-hour traffic, so I told Rolly that I'd stay behind and read for another hour. The library was open until 7:00, anyway.

Rolly said we should take a walk. The school campus was next to the bay, between a hospital and the old Wicker estate abandoned since World War II. A shallow creek separated the school from the estate at one end of the campus. Rolly took me to where the creek opened to the bay and we sat on the seawall and looked out at the water.

I liked the quiet. The people I knew dreaded silence. They had loud music going all the time or talked nonstop or had the loud music going and talked nonstop over it. Sitting next to Rolly, not saying anything, listening to the sound of the dragonflies and the bay water slapping the seawall, made me feel like time had stopped.

Then Rolly leaned over and put his arm over my shoulders. I put my hand on his thigh.[5] And when I raised my face, he kissed me.

He kept his eyes closed and tipped his head a few degrees in each direction, the way people do in movies. So I closed my eyes, too.

He leaned closer. I felt the tip of his tongue try to push past my lips, but I wouldn't open them. Not yet. Instead, I kept thinking about what my Biology teacher said.

---

5. From my previous one and only boyfriend, and from Mr. Hackett's Biology class the year before, I knew that by putting my hand on his thigh I was signaling my acceptance of his advance. Mr. Hackett said, "Don't fool yourselves, guys. It's the female of the species that's always in control."

An hour later, we were sitting in his car, parked in one of the student lots, still kissing. My lips and my jaw began to hurt, the way your feet hurt when you're breaking in new shoes. I was ready to go further, so I took his hand and placed it over my left breast. He took my hand and placed it over his you-know-what, which embarrassed me because I had never before put my hand anywhere near a guy's you-know-what, but I was going to be mature about this.

A custodian tapped on Rolly's window and told us we had to move because it was 6:00 and he was locking the gate. Now I was really embarrassed. Rolly thanked the man and called him "sir," and, once he closed his window, whistled all the way to the other end of the lot, where my car was parked. For a few days after that, I couldn't stop thinking about it.

9. WHAT'S THE BIG DEAL WITH SEX, ANYWAY?

My parents like to sleep in late on Sunday mornings, so I slip into the kitchen downstairs and get a Coke from the refrigerator and a bag of Brussels cookies out of the cupboard. But for my father's sweet tooth, we'd be eating nuts and berries. My mother has this silly notion that sodas are bad for you because they're not natural, like orange or apple juice. If she catches me drinking one, especially for breakfast, she'll do a Fidel and switch into harangue mode. Castro is renowned for being able to talk nonstop for hours. He has nothing on my mother, though, who can do that and return to the point. "Anything natural is always better for you," she'll say. And I'll counter, "Curare's natural too." "You know what I meant," she'll say, but it's too late. She falls for it every time.

Back in my room, I turn on the TV and leave it on mute. I think about what I don't want to think about, what I've been thinking about all morning when I should have been thinking about something else. I can't believe Rolly would give up what we had together for a sleazy bitch like Lizette. She's such a phony, too. Her name's not even

Lizette. Her real name is Luz Isabel. But she hates it, so she made up the "Lizette" part. The first day of class each year, we go through the same routine—Lizette correcting the teacher reading off the class roll. "Not Luz," she says, "It's Lizette—one zee and two tees." Mr. Hackett used to make fun of her. He called her Two Tees. I think Luz fits her better, not because it means "light" in Spanish, but because it sounds like what she is. (Har. Har.)

I've known Lizette since first grade. A whole bunch of us have been going to the same private schools for years. She's always been a troublemaker, talking back to teachers, wearing her school uniform way above her knees. In eighth grade, she was caught smoking in the girls' bathroom. The following year, she started sleeping around. In tenth grade, she was popping ecstasy and drinking vodka. The rumor was that she got pregnant and had an abortion. This year, she claims to know one of the guys who works at Alchemy, the dance club on South Beach. The guy's supposed to be, like, twenty-two. I don't talk to Lizette. Teri talks to her, then tells us about it at lunch or when we go out. Lizette knows I can't stand her. She tells Teri that I'm envious because I can't get into Alchemy. Like I care.

By now, you must be asking yourself—where are this girl's parents? Seven years ago, when Lizette was ten, her father committed suicide. He was a bank president or maybe he really owned the bank, as Lizette claims. (You can't believe anything she says.) One thing is true. I know because it was on TV and everybody, my parents, even the nuns at school, talked about it: Just before they found her father hanging from a tree over a bus stop in Key Biscayne, the police in Miami arrested a former Central American president who had stolen something like a billion dollars from his country's treasury and fled to a two-story penthouse on Brickell. The ex-president confessed that a great deal of the money had been deposited in Lizette's father's bank. All that was in the news. Shortly after, a group of kids waiting for the school bus smelled something rotten, looked up, and discovered her father's body hanging from a tree branch, a rope tied around his neck, one foot still wearing an expensive Italian loafer.

Lizette's mother lost everything—the house, the cars. She became a drunk and a Darvocet addict, did some rehab, married a local radio personality, then was in the news again when she burned down his house and brought charges against him for molesting Lizette when she was fourteen. The charges were never proven and the radio personality got off, but my mother said that he had the best criminal lawyer in town. I forget his lawyer's name right now, but he's on *Court TV* all the time.

As a result of her father's suicide and her mother's going off the deep end, the nuns at the school feel sorry for Lizette. She always gets detention, no matter the offense, when anyone else would have been suspended. A lot of the time, the nuns and teachers simply look the other way. Which is why she still wears the shortest skirts in the school. And when she climbs the stairs between classes, a gaggle of guys, usually freshman, follow her half a flight behind.

The rumor is that she's done most of the guys in our class (probably an exaggeration), that the sex is porno-raunchy (possible), that she's a nympho (definitely). Which leads me to the next point—

What does Rolly see in Lizette? Even if she gives him all the sex he wants, and he always wanted it, I can't picture them together. She's half a head taller than he is. Her hair is a permanent shade of burnt copper with black roots from all the different things she's done to it. Her eyes can be blue, purple, or feline yellow, depending on which colored contacts she's wearing. She has the Chinese character for "joy" tattooed below her panty line, which she's shown to everyone in gym. Lizette doesn't care if her hose have a run going up the entire length of her leg. And she's come to class smelling of cigarettes and alcohol. She's loud, too, like when she blurted out in Health class that she swallows.

Rolly, on the other hand, is sooooo picky. He has a rule about everything. Open his school locker and you'll find his textbooks arranged in alphabetical order by subject. If Rolly and Lizette were stranded on a deserted island in the middle of the Pacific with absolutely no hope of ever being rescued, I picture Rolly running away from her, to the other side of the island.

What's the big deal with sex, anyway? Me? I prefer curling up with a good book.

10. ONE WORD FITS ALL

I sit up in bed, cross my legs, and balance the laptop on my thighs. Maybe I should have traded my topic with Mariella. I could have distracted myself thinking about the virtues, the necessity, of honesty. It's one of those qualities that's so simple you can even write a utilitarian argument to support it. The world would simply break down if everyone were dishonest all the time. "Love," on the other hand, like "art" or "cancer," is a word that stands for many different things.

There's guy-and-girl love. There's love for your friends, your family, your parents, love for your country, too. At school, Brother Richard talks to us about love for God, but I think that's mostly fear, like when you're doing something you shouldn't be doing and all the while you're being watched by tiny hidden cameras.[6]

When I think about plain, old, generic love, I think of my parents. My father's a doctor, a psychiatrist. My mom's an attorney. She writes wills for people that their relatives can argue about later. My parents grew up in Miami, after their parents brought them over from Cuba when they were two or something, because of the whole Fidel thing. They met in grade school. Kids in those days went through some pretty scary drills in the middle of the day. The principal made an announcement over the PA, and the nuns said things

---

6. In freshman year, Gloria and I once skipped class after lunch and took the train to the mall. We chose an empty car. No sooner had Gloria put her feet up on the seat across from her than a voice boomed over the loudspeakers telling her to take her feet down. "I'm talking to you, young lady," the voice said. That freaked us out. I think God's like that, without the speakers.

like, "OK, children, now get under your desks." And my mom and dad, only they weren't my mom and dad yet, they were little kids, crawled under their desks in case the Russians dropped a hydrogen bomb on Miami. I've tried to imagine what a classroom full of children crouching under wooden desks would have looked like. I've tried to imagine what they thought about, practicing for the end of the world. As bad as things are today, I can't imagine growing up like that.

My parents married right out of high school, which is one thing they both agree no one should ever do, except them, of course. Their situation was different, my father told me at dinner one evening. They started to go steady in tenth grade, which in those days meant they could go to the beach with a group of friends or to the movies if my mother's grandmother, who died before I was born, chaperoned them. Cubans were really big into that in the 1960s and 1970s, when my parents were kids. My father said his parents didn't leave Cuba, they brought it with them. My mother said Cubans in 1970s Miami were still living in 1950s Havana.

I used to think all men were like my father. I know that's kind of classic. One day, when I was about four years old and my mother was working late, I asked my father to marry me. He told me that parents could never marry their children. Why not? I asked. "Because *their* children would have watermelons for heads and claws instead of hands," he said. You should never tell a child something like that. I imagined the watermelon children crawling out from under my bed, their monstrous heads tipping perilously on thin necks, claws snapping in the air above me, while I lay covered to my eyes under one of my mother's precious Egyptian-cotton, don't-you-dare-stain-it bed sheets. For months, I had to sleep with Nana. My father, of all people, should have known better.

All this came up again at dinner not long ago. We were talking about marriage—why some worked and many did not. Well, my parents were talking about it. I listened, mostly. The only thing I said was that I wanted to find someone like my dad. I thought the comment would earn me some good favor, to be cashed in at the appropriate time. Instead, it led to the recounting of the watermelon children story (anything to embarrass Silvia). My father said that I would make up my own mind about men in general and about the kind of man I wanted for myself specifically. "You'll need a companion," he said. "Almost everyone does." "Companion," to me, means someone who goes along with you on a short trip, two little old ladies sitting next to each other on a tour bus rubbernecking past the Eiffel Tower. My father thinks marriage is feudal, that women should be self-sufficient, so they never have to stay with a man they don't love anymore or one who is abusive. "Everything in its good time," he says.

The first thing my parents want me to do is get an education. They want me to become a doctor, maybe a cancer doctor or a surgeon. I'm not sure medicine is for me. You get to do cool stuff like talk to a family about the dying relative you're treating, while they hang on your every word, but I'm sure that gets old. My father says that whatever I do, I should get an education so I can have my own paycheck. "Don't let those nuns at school convince you that money isn't important," my father says, jamming a thumb into the air. "If they really believed that, they wouldn't be forcing us to buy all those candy bars."

I think my parents are happy being married to each other. My father makes funny faces at my mother at the dinner table, and more than once I've caught her squeezing his thigh, which really embarrasses me. I've tried to ask them if they had sex before they got married. I'm almost sure they did. Didn't they grow up in a time when everyone was sleeping around? But as I start to ask them, I get embarrassed and let the moment pass. My father says I can talk to him about anything I want, but he's a guy. I'd prefer to talk with my mother, except she can be such a logarithmic dork.

My parents grew up believing that the one sure way to happiness and satisfaction is through education. I don't think they really believe that anymore, seeing as the world has changed so much since they were my age, and both lawyers and doctors are dropping out to do things like run bookstores and sail around the world. But my parents want to play it safe, so they tell me the same thing their parents told them: "You never know."

My parents say it in English. My grandparents use the Spanish. *Uno nunca sabe.* One never knows. It's shorthand for "Look what happened to us." It means that they went from living one life in 1950s Cuba to another in 1960s Miami, that doctors, lawyers, and bankers were forced to take jobs as busboys, waiters, and house-keepers at the Eden Roc and the Shelborne hotels, that families were separated, sometimes never to speak again, that Havana would begin its slow descent into becoming a pile of old stones, one crumbling balcony at a time.

It also means that everyone lives in two places at once—the present here and the past there. The past was once a common ground that all Cuban exiles shared, even people like my parents, who spent their entire lives in Miami, but that is not true so much anymore. The old Cubans who left in the 1950s distrust the new Cubans who grew up under communism. My grandfather complains that the new Cubans are snitches and come here looking for a handout. They leech off the government. "That's all they've ever known," he says. The word "exile" underlines how Miami Cubans see themselves. The second worst thing you can call an exile is "refugee."

That's another kind of love that I can write about in my essay— the love of country. You say "country" and most people think of a colored patch on a map. "Country" for me means New Year's Eve at my grandfather's house, roast pork with mojito barbecue sauce, my grandmother's white rice and black beans seasoned with just the right amount of cumin. It means sweet plantains and my mother's pumpkin flan.

11. THE WAR OF MY GRANDMOTHER'S BLACK BEANS

Like any country, this one has its own customs. I have to tell my grandmother that she makes the best black beans in the universe. I have to serve myself twice, at least, or risk igniting a cultural war. If

I don't exhaust every hyperbole to describe her black beans and I haven't served myself to the point at which I'm forced to unsnap my jeans under the table, my grandmother will say, "*Ay*, Silvita doesn't like the food." Once she does that, it's too late. There's no turning back. Getting up for a second helping at that point won't help. It's the first volley in the war, a battle cry to my grandfather, who then pipes up about the loss of Cuban values among the Youth of Today.

"No, no, no, no," my grandmother says, her voice running up a scale of notes, flicking her hand, as if the situation were beyond critical, "they don't even speak Spanish anymore."

From the specific—*you don't like my black beans*—my grandparents extract the general—*you reject your Cuban roots*. From the individual—*you look down on the Cuban*—they get the universal—*your entire generation despises everything Cuban, thus assuring the Imminent Demise of Civilization as We Know It.*

My father used to intervene about this point. He tried to assure his parents that things were not as bad as they thought, but that only made my grandparents turn all their guns on him and his "psychiatric ways." In fact, my grandfather, who retired from his cardiology practice ten years ago, believes psychiatrists and their ilk are the cause of Everything That Is Wrong in the World. (My grandparents talk like that, using a lot of capital letters.) Now my father knows better, so he remains quiet.

Then my grandparents set out to prove the superiority of their own times. My grandfather says to me, "You think that you are living in a better world because you have a computer (a word he says in English) and a fancy German car and your own color TV." My grandmother follows with "Remember those beautiful boleros, Fito?"

"They were healthy diversions," my grandfather says, picking up the pace.

"Now all they have—"

"Is that . . . what do you call it?"

"Rrrrap," my grandmother says, trilling the r's.

"I don't understand how anyone can listen to that, that—"

"It's unspeakable," my grandmother says with such force that her dentures come loose.

Then my grandfather, eighty years old, very thin, with white hair and wire-rimmed glasses, bobs back and forth in his chair at the head of the table, puffing his cheeks, moving his hands in the air, making mock gang signs with his fingers, the knuckles of which are thick and knobby.

My mother laughs.

My father says, "Oh, please."

I know better than to say anything.

"That is what your generation calls art," my grandmother says, introducing the next phase in the war.

My grandfather pushes himself away from the table, grabs his cane, and walks to the Florida room, a large, tiled room with a ceiling fan, a wet bar, and an old console stereo, where he keeps his LPs.

My mother uses the interruption to pick up the plates and serve her pumpkin flan, which is my favorite part of the meal. And while we wait, my grandfather plays his LPs on the stereo, the TV on mute and tuned to Times Square, so we can watch the stupid ball drop at midnight. Logarithmic dorkiness, I know, but it's not my show. He plays boleros sung by the stars of their generation, their times, their country. He also plays mambos, *son montunos*, and Cuban big band music, all of it way too loud. It's no use asking him to turn it down. He stands by the stereo, one hand on his cane, the other pointing at the record, his mouth forming the words. "What do you think of that, eh?"

My mother motions me to help with the dishes. My grandmother waves everyone to sit down. My grandfather, after dessert and a few more Scotches, takes my grandmother's hand and they dance. I'd never seen anyone dance holding a cane, but my grandfather is so good, he uses it to pivot while dancing a merengue. My mother takes a picture of them and blinds everyone with the flashbulb.

Then midnight arrives and the stupid Times Square ball drops slowly and everyone kisses everyone else and stuffs their mouths with twelve grapes, one each time the big clock in the hall chimes, one grape after another, for good luck, and my grandmother opens the front door and throws a bucket of water down the front steps so she can start off clean for the new year and, later, when my grandfather has once again checked to make sure that everyone's drink is topped off and he's finally turned down the music, he'll make a toast. "Next year in Havana," he says, the glass held in front of him, his head bowed slightly.

Years later, when I look at the picture of my grandparents dancing, it will be that moment that I will think of as my country, my own corner of the world, from which time and circumstances will inevitably make of me one more exile.

12. NÚÑEZ'S LAW OF PREDICTABLE UNPREDICTABILITY

It isn't like Rolly and I didn't almost do it. More than once, we got very close to going all the way. Each time, I pushed him back at the last moment, which led to a cascade of reactions by Rolly, beginning with surprise, progressing to pleading, concluding with irritation.

Rolly had to have it. He had one thing on his mind. He was all hands, all the time. "No, Rolly!" I said. It was funny at first. It tickled. But when we went out and he didn't let me watch the movie, I got mad. What was the point of going to a movie if you weren't going to watch it. "Stop it!" I said, pointing a finger at Rolly, the way you do with a puppy.

Rolly didn't stop. He slipped his hand down my bra, squeezed my breasts until they hurt, and tried to get the other hand between my legs. "Stop it, Rolly!" Sometimes I wished I were like that Indian goddess with all the arms, so I could fend him off.

Rolly had five excuses for his behavior that he used in no discernable order—

♂ "But it's natural."

♂ "I thought you wanted it too."

♂ "We've been going out for almost a whole week."

♂ "Are you frigid?"

♂ "They hurt. If I don't get it soon, they'll explode."

Maybe Rolly and I would have gone all the way if he hadn't been so insistent. There's no better way to turn me off to something than to keep bringing it up. But it wasn't only his insistence that made me resist him; it's also that sex can be messy, dangerous too.

Last week, Mr. Pennington in Health class showed us a really gross video about sexually transmitted diseases, some of which have no cure. They are, like, forever. There were pictures: A woman who looked as if she were giving birth to a giant cauliflower. Another of genitals that were raw and blistery red. An emaciated man who looked like a prisoner in a death camp. "And don't think that it can't happen to you, that it only happens to the homeless or to drug addicts. It happens to kids like you all the time," Mr. Pennington said. He picked up the textbook and held it a few inches above his desk. The book was the same one Rudy Menocal tried to steal last quarter to get the answers to a quiz we were having the next morning. As soon as Mr. Pennington stepped out of the classroom, Rudy ran up to the desk and opened the book. The only problem was that Mr. Pennington returned sooner than expected and caught Rudy going through the answers. He could have had Rudy expelled, but Mr. P.'s a nice guy. Instead, he spoke to Rudy's parents, who took his car away from him for the rest of the school year.[7] Rudy takes the school

---

7. Having a car, in high school anyway, is what economists call an "intangible value." It raises a person's value in the eyes of his peers. Mr. Núñez says it's the unpredictability of human behavior that keeps economics from being a real science, like physics. If human beings were only more rational, he says, economists could run the world efficiently. Mr. Núñez wears clip-on ties that don't always match his short-sleeved shirts. One of his favorite words is "pomposity." Driving a big SUV is a pomposity, he says. So is paying athletes millions of dollars to play children's games. One day, he got into it with Alvaro Aróstegui. Alvaro is the school's best pitcher and running back, and he's pretty good at track too. Everybody says he's going to be a big star one day.

bus, but it hasn't made him any less obnoxious. You'd think he were still driving his little silver Lexus, offering girls rides home, like Erin Guterson, who models swimwear for a local department store, though I think she likes girls more than she likes boys because I've caught her looking at me in the locker room. Anyway, Mr. Pennington picked up the book, held it in the air for a moment for dramatic effect, and let it fall on the desk. And when he did that, the book went boom!

A few girls jumped. One of the guys said "co-ñó," which is a Cuban curse word you hear a lot in Miami and which has no equivalent in English. But Mr. Pennington didn't lose a beat, in part, I think, because he is already half-Cubanized himself. He married a Cuban woman ten years older than him, who owns a big apartment building that she inherited from her last husband. Plus I've seen Mr. P. drink *cafecitos* with Ms. Rodriguez after lunch in the teachers' lounge. She's the young French teacher with the face like the Madonna who recently got her Ph.D. from Columbia. People say there's something going on between them, but I think Mr. P. is a super-nice guy, so it's no wonder Ms. Rodriguez has *cafecitos* with him. That day in class, when he dropped the book on the desk for dramatic effect, he waited a couple of seconds before he said it again. "Don't think that it can't happen to you."

Now here comes the irrational part, the part that my AP Economics teacher says makes his job and the job of economists the world over so much harder than it needs to be, the part he calls the "predictable unpredictability of the human animal's insistence on pursuing inscrutable ends for unknowable reasons."[8] In spite of everything, my trampled ego, my mother's advice, Mr. Pennington's video with people growing weird stuff from their genitals, I am sure that if Rolly called me right now to get back together with him, I'd not only say yes, I'd get in my car, drive over to his house, and let him go all

---

8. Mr. Filisberto Núñez, AP Economics Class, Room 702, Academy of Saint Thomas the Apostle, Miami, February 23, 10:42 A.M.

the way. I know this sounds like a contradiction, especially after what I told you about Mr. Pennington and his warts-and-sores show. But, like Mr. Núñez says, people don't always do the rational thing.

13. THE THINKING WOMAN'S GUIDE TO TANGAS AND CELLULITE

I spend the rest of the morning working on my essay. It occurs to me that love, of whatever kind, is not eternal. It can't be. How many songs go something like "I'll love you till the end of time"? But love is not a "thing" or a "force" that exists independently of the host or the object. John cannot love Mary after John is dead, nor can he love her after Mary is dead. If John survives Mary, he may love her memory, but that is something else. Because love resides in us, it is dependent on us.

It gets worse. Even if John and Mary love each other for many years, everybody changes over time. John and Mary are not the same people five, ten, twenty-five years after the day they first fell in love. When they change, their love, too, being dependent on them, has to change. I know this sounds nitpicky, but it's not beside the point.

When I was a child, my father kept a chart of my growth. He measured my height every six months. He says that I will continue to develop until I'm in my early twenties, a good thing too, I think, because I am too skinny. Francesca Gutierrez's parents nixed her getting a boob job, which she wanted instead of a car for her birthday last year. The doctor said she had not yet fully developed and he didn't want to operate on her until then. On the other hand, Gloria is what you could call prematurely well developed. She was the first in the class to get her period when we were eleven years old. She has a perfect hourglass figure. When we go out, guys ogle her. I'd like to look a little more like that, but then I remind myself that she'll probably be fat in ten years. Girls like that peak at fifteen and it's downhill from there. If I were a guy, and if I were in love with the present-day shapely Gloria, I think it would be real tough to stay in love with her, as I watched her balloon. To survive such extravagant metamorphosis, love has to find something other than the physical to attach itself to, maybe her personality, I don't know.

Which leads me to my next point: love takes work. Ignore it, and it will die. My mother likes to say, "Out of sight, out of mind." She clears her life of a lot of what she calls "distractions" that way. She tells me that part of maturing is being able to focus on what is important and letting go of what is not. "There are only so many hours in the day." For that, she says, you have to love yourself.

Some people think you have to love yourself before you can love anyone else, that love of self is a prerequisite, like taking Algebra 1 before they let you take Algebra 2. But love of self can be tricky. You are never just one person. There's the one you see in the mirror. There's another that my friends see at school. And another that my parents see at home. There's the self who is working on Mrs. Eden's extra-credit essay on love. There's the other self who is sitting on my bed, thinking about this. And so on. If we take this notion—self-love —to it's logical conclusion, as Rolly would say, then I can never truly love myself, not only because I have so many selves, but also because each self is constantly changing.

Let's take an easy one—love of the self you see in the mirror. It's timely too because summer break is around the corner. Summer means the beach. The beach means bathing suits. It means, in a word, exposure.

I am fascinated with tangas. Every time I see a model wearing one in a magazine, I keep coming back to the page. I realize that I could never wear one, even to lie by our pool at home. My father would shut himself in his study. My mother would come outside. "Let me explain something," she would say, closing the sliding glass doors behind her.

For these reasons, wearing a tanga to me represents emancipation because someday I'll be able to wear one regardless of my parents' opinion on the matter. It represents liberation, too, because someday, perhaps, I'll have the nerve to wear one, even if I don't have the body for it. It represents independence, the absence of any need to rely on what others think of me.

On South Beach, I've seen fat and painfully pale middle-aged women wear tangas. They proclaim their confidence by traveling halfway around the globe to bare themselves in one of the world's great capitals of vanity. Here I am, they seem to say, with no concern if anyone notices. Here I am, they say, because I don't need you to tell me what I look like.

I am what I am, they declare with every step, even as the fat in their thighs dimples.

I'd like to be able to do that someday, turn my back on the beach and look out to the horizon, as far as I can see, without caring what anyone thinks of my body or about me. Here I am, I'll say to myself. Here and now, I am.

14. AFTER WORKING ON HER ESSAY FOR MRS. EDEN, SILVIA SPENDS THE AFTERNOON WITH HER PARENTS AND GRANDPARENTS, AND ON THE WAY BACK HOME SHE SENDS ROLLY AN ILL-CONCEIVED CONCILIATORY TEXT MESSAGE

lets talk? :-)

15. GIRLS MEET GUYS

Sunday night. I definitely do not want to stay in. Gloria's already made plans with Teri O'Donnell, and, again, she hasn't invited me, nor does she invite me now that I'm talking to her on the phone and asking, almost insisting, to go along. Ignoring all my manners I say, "Good, where can I meet up with you guys?"

I meet them on Lincoln Road, at a café not far from Meridian Avenue. Gloria and Teri sit very close to each other, like two people whispering secrets.

The waitress lights the candle in the middle of the table. Gloria orders a Cosmopolitan and gets away with it. Teri orders the same. I ask for a Coke.

Teri's trying to convince us to go with her to some strip mall church she's joined, one of those Bible-thumping cults that's all about hell and donations. Gloria pretends to be interested, but I know she's just being nice.

So I'm listening to Teri go on about John this and Revelations that when I notice a guy at the table next to ours staring at me. He's sitting with two other guys. They look old, nineteen or twenty, but they're drinking beer, so maybe they are even older. The guy who's staring at me is not bad-looking. Sandy blond hair. Can't tell the color of his eyes. He's wearing a dark tee shirt with something written in what looks like Japanese, blue jeans, and Adidas sneakers. He's got his legs stretched out from under the table. The waitress comes by holding a tray of drinks and almost trips over the guy's feet. She stops, points at his feet, and he draws them in. He looks like he's apologizing to her. Then he looks at me, shrugs his shoulder, and smiles. I turn away.

Teri's telling Gloria that she has to save herself. You have to *save* yourself, she says, which sounds like Teri, drama queen. Last year she wanted to convert us all to the Carbo/Turbo Diet. You're supposed to lose ten pounds in ten days. Even after the guy who wrote the book got sued when someone who went on the diet died of a massive heart attack and all his books were pulled off bookstore shelves, Teri insisted that it had worked for her and we absolutely needed it, never mind the implications behind the "needed it" part. She's stubborn like that. Like the way she's plucked out her eyebrows and drawn them back on with a pencil. (What's with that?) Everyone tells her she has a "pronounced" forehead ("pronounced" being the polite word for "huge"—Rudy calls her "Billboard"), so she doesn't need to highlight it some more by drawing in pencil-thin eyebrows. Do you think she listens to us?

It bothers me a little that Gloria went out with Teri again tonight and didn't invite me. Especially to South Beach, which Gloria knows is, like, my favorite place in the world. The way Gloria and Teri talk to each other, you'd think they were best friends. Only last month at lunch, Gloria said that Teri walks like a horse and the whole table laughed, so I don't understand the origins of this newfound friendship.

Teri hangs out mostly with Francesca Gutierrez. All year, they've been skipping class at least once a week to smoke in the Moon Temple on the old Wicker estate next to the school. The grounds of the abandoned estate are overgrown, and the fountains are green with algae and smell like rotten eggs. I went there once, with Gloria, exploring. The place isn't really a temple, but a two-story building that looks like it used to be the gardener's quarters. The front door's gone, and most of the windowpanes are broken. Someone years ago named it the Moon Temple. It was around even before my parents went to school there. No one knows why they call it that, though there are jokes about what the "Moon" part really means. It's the place where Sister Edna and, before her, a coach who retired a long time ago and who's probably dead by now, assured their place in school history by catching several couples going all the way. Every summer, the school mends the fence that runs from the creek to the highway. The metal sign that reads NO TRESPASSING in faded red letters is replaced with a freshly painted one. Then someone tears a new hole in the fence and it's a free-for-all until the next couple is caught. Most of the time Sister Edna catches the unlucky couple walking over there or coming back. At least they have their clothes on. Two years ago, she caught a couple *in flagrante delicto*, which is Latin for "deep doo-doo." They were in another class so I didn't know them, but the rumor is that the girl was lying under the guy, oohing and aahing, while he was going at it, and when the girl opened her eyes, she saw Sister Edna's watery eyes squinting behind thick wire-frame glasses, peering over the guy's shoulder. Both the girl and the guy were expelled the same day. The rumor went through the whole school, via text messaging. The Moon Temple was off-limits again. The building was boarded up and the chainlink fence repaired.

Most of the time, though, it's cat and mouse, with the mice getting away with it. You have to be into weird things to take off your clothes in all that filth. Almost everyone has a car so it isn't like you don't have a cleaner place to do it. Maybe it's the rush of doing it under the school's collective and official noses. Some people get off on that. I kind of expect the nuns to bulldoze the Moon Temple one day, but it's on private property. My mother says the Moon Temple is what in the law they call an "attractive nuisance," which sounds cool, like the name of a new band.

But now Teri and Gloria have this newfound friendship, and they're talking to each other like I don't exist.

I take my phone out of my purse and check for messages. None.

The guy at the table, the one with the sandy blond hair, is trying to get my attention. I can feel him looking at me, so I concentrate on the flip-open keyboard of the phone. Maybe Rolly hasn't looked at his messages. He isn't very diligent about that, which could explain why he hasn't texted back or called me.

My phone chirps. For an instant I think it's Rolly. I close the keyboard and press Send.

"Where are you?" my mother says.

I tell her.

"Who else is there?"

I tell her that too.

"Make sure you get back before eleven. You have school tomorrow."

"I know," I say, before I press End. I look at my watch—9:25 P.M.

I flip open the keyboard again. What if Mr. Núñez is wrong? What if the law of supply and demand does not apply to love? Look at Lizette—any more supply, and she'll run out of herself. On the other hand, maybe I've made myself so rare that I've priced myself out of the market. Or maybe love is neither a good nor a service, but its own raison d'être, needing no justification. It simply is.

miss u :-(

I type and scroll down until I've got Rolly's number.

"Hi," the sandy blond–haired guy says. He's standing in front of me. "Do you mind if I sit?" He sounds English or Dutch or maybe Danish.

Gloria and Teri stop talking and look at the guy. I press Send and shut the keyboard.

16. THE OTHER FISH IN THE OCEAN

Fifteen minutes later, Michael, the sandy blond–haired guy, and his friends Alan and Peter are sitting at our table, ordering drinks for everyone. I stick with my soda. They are from the U.K. Two of them were admitted to Cambridge, one to the University of London. They are here for the summer. Alan is very thin, nerdy, with dark hair and glasses. Peter is stocky and reminds me a little of Rolly in the way he dresses. He is the only one wearing an actual shirt instead of a tee shirt. His father, Michael tells us, is rich to an unseemly degree and owns a condo on South Beach, right on the beach, which is when I think that the next thing they'll be doing is inviting us to see the old man's watercolor collection.

Gloria likes Alan. She does not take her eyes off him. Teri looks annoyed for having lost the opportunity to proselytize. I'm a little nervous. I'm not naturally outgoing, especially with guys who are older, come from a place that's thousands of miles away, and have accents that make their banter sound like a comedy routine, so you don't know when they're serious.

Earlier this year, when I first started to think about college, I realized that it would be my chance to leave home and still be under my parents' care. What better deal could anyone ask for? You get the freedom of being on your own, all expenses paid. I asked for brochures from universities in Europe because I thought it would be an elegant thing to be able to say that you studied there, plus they have nice-looking diplomas in ancient languages. (My gynecologist graduated from the University of Bologna.) In the end, though, I knew it would have to be the United States, probably California, if I wanted to go somewhere far from home.

Meeting Michael and his friends reminded me how much change there would be in my life in the coming year. After these two weeks of finals, there'd be the summer, then senior year—standardized tests and college applications. Then I'd be gone. So why bother with Rolly or anyone else? If we got serious, we'd only have to break up the following year. I've heard about long-distance relationships, and they don't work. So why not focus on school? Go out occasionally, but never, ever let it get past the most casual kind of kissing. None of the heavy stuff, like what happened with Rolly.

Then I hear Michael asking me what I'm thinking about.

"Probably her boyfriend," Teri says.

"Ex-boyfriend," Gloria says.

"Ex-boyfriend? Poor guy," Michael says. He turns to me. "I hope you let him down easy. He must be crushed."

"He dumped her," Teri says.

I look at Teri, hoping she'll turn into a pile of salt.

"Then he's a wanker," Peter says.

Gloria, Teri, and I look at one another. No one wants to admit that we don't know what that word means.

"A jerk-off, in your language," Peter adds.

"Don't mind Peter," Michael says. "His dad's counting on me to polish his manners, teach him the essentials, like which fork's for the salad and which one's for the main dish. Like not picking his nose in public. The basics of social intercourse amongst civilized peoples."

Peter's about to say something when the waitress reappears with another round of drinks. Teri lights a cigarette and hands it to Gloria, who smokes it like she's been smoking her whole life. I try to get her attention because I know my face is saying *Since when have you been smoking cigarettes?* but she keeps her eyes on Alan, who is lighting a brand of cigarettes I've never heard of. He offers everyone a cigarette, including me.

"Christ, Alan," Peter says, fanning the air in front of his face. "I thought you'd outgrown your Jean-Paul Belmondo stage."

"His what?" Gloria asks.

"The French actor," Peter says.

"Pay no attention to my provincial friends. They grew up on meat and potatoes," Alan says after exhaling for what seems like a very long time.

"Not *boeuf* and *pommes de terre*, like Alain here," Peter says.

"They're just jealous of my cosmopolitan upbringing," Alan says, looking at me.

I do the polite thing and smile, though I'm calculating whether I'll be home by 11:00 and my mind is playing a scene in which my mother grounds me until the next sighting of Halley's comet.

"It smells like you've ignited a pile of yak dung," Peter says.

The topic of conversation changes from the differences between American and European attitudes toward smoking to the differences in musical tastes. I admit I've never heard of the band Alan's talking about, so he offers to lend me the CD.

"Mosh's last CD's brilliant!" he says.

"Definitely," Gloria says, like she knows what she's talking about, "brilliant!"

Gloria says, "Hey, Alan, what do you think of Miami?" or something like that, which makes him say, "Well, very beautiful, I think," while he is looking at me, making my ears feel hot, making me pick up the drinks menu from the center of the table, next to the candle, and pretend to read it.

"You're not going to drink, are you?" Teri says.

"Sister Mary Magdalene here?" Gloria says, pointing at me with her thumb. Teri laughs. Now I'm thinking Rudy's right, her forehead does look like a billboard.

I know Gloria's mad at me because of what Alan said. She's used to being the absolute center of attention with guys. And she's twice as mad because she likes Alan.

For a second, I wish Alan hadn't said that or that he'd directed his

comment to Gloria, not me. That's for a second. Then the wish evap-
orates faster than the foam on the lip of the ocean. And my ears cool
off. I imagine Alan and Michael and—why not?—Peter too, ogling
me. I imagine an entire neighborhood of guys I've never met calling
me to ask me out, filling up my voice mail with messages of desperate and unrequited love, palpable and undeniable *want*, painful and
desperate confessions that I am the unmovable center of their lives.
I imagine that Rolly calls, but when he does the voice mail is full and
a recording informs his broken heart that my cell phone is not ac-
cepting any more messages, *his* especially.

Too late, I think. I imagine myself telling him off when he catches
up to me between classes, my books held against my chest to keep
him from getting too close, to stop all attempts at reconciliation. Too
late. You could have had me, Rolly. Instead you went for the lowest
common denominator with Lizette. Too, too late.

"Sorry?" Michael says, leaning close to me, so I can hear him
above the noise.

That's when I feel someone lightly tap the tops of my toes, like a
signal from the other end of the universe. *Tap-tap. Tap-tap.*

Should I draw my feet under my chair? Should I tap back and, if
so, what should I tap—the prime numbers, like some kind of Project
SETI? 1, 3, 5, 7. 1, 3, 5, 7.

Michael's turned away, listening to Teri talk about the end of the
world. I look around the table for a hint about the identity of the foot
tapper. The table's small enough that anyone, even the shortest
among us, can extend a leg and reach the person at the diametrically
opposite side. Gloria has her eyes fixed on Alan. She holds the hand
with the lit cigarette up against her face, the tip of her pinky tracing
the outline of her lips. I'm sure she learned that from an actress in a
movie. This is sooooo not like Gloria. Her eyes are squinting from
the smoke rising off the end of her cigarette. She says, "Teri, let's talk
about something else."

"No, it's quite interesting," Peter says. "Really."

"I'd like to know how it'll all end," Alan says.

But Teri gets the message. She stops talking and slouches back in her chair, arms across her chest, her forehead shiny with perspiration. Peter's looking at Gloria when he's not fanning the smoke coming off Alan's cigarette. A sweat spot, shaped like a crescent moon, appears on the front of his shirt between his belly and his chest. Alan catches me looking and winks.

I think it's him tapping. Then the tapping stops. And before I can react, Alan turns to Gloria and engages in frank and flagrant flirting. This is very confusing. Maybe it's a foreign thing. He reaches across the table to Gloria and places his hand on hers.

"Aren't we getting a bit chummy?" Peter says.

"Mind your manners," Michael says.

Alan pulls his hand back.

"Unlike Michael here, who is all ciphers and formulas," Alan says, "I'm no cold fish."

"Don't mind him," Michael says. "He's jealous because he was never any good at maths, which explains why he's going to read English."

"They're all ponces in English anyway, aren't they?" Peter says.

The waitress comes by with another round of drinks. When she leaves, I ask—

"Is Michael a cold fish?" Everyone looks at me, making me wish I hadn't said that.

"Well," I say, deciding it's too late to turn back now, "are you a cold fish?"

Peter says, "Alan speaks metaphorically. Michael possesses one of the finest minds since Newton and one of the warmest hearts since Keats."

"'Ode on a Grecian Urn,'" I blurt out. I look at the glass of Coke and wonder if someone spiked it.

"Exactly," Peter says. "Michael here is Isaac Keats."

Michael says, "I'm not entirely about numbers."

I wish I had a bon mot, but nothing comes to mind, except the lyrics of "Throbbin' Like an Aneurysm," which for some unknowable reason is playing in my mind and I can't turn it off. My father says that a conversation should be like a tennis match, the ball always in play, floating back and forth over the net. I've just watched the ball fly past me. So I pick up my glass and take a sip to occupy my hands.

Alan says, "Anyone fancy a walk on the beach?"

My chance, I think, to call it a night. But before I can protest about the time—it is midnight and I know that I'm already in big trouble at home—Gloria says, "Sounds good to me." Teri nods.

What's gotten into Gloria? She has a curfew like mine. Teri too. To complicate things, while we're waiting for the check, my mother texts me.

Is everything OK? Why aren't you home?

That's just like my mother to use proper punctuation. I text her back.

totally ok b home soon

And I hope she doesn't call. With text messaging you can limit the communication. On the phone, talking, she'll ask me a bunch of annoying questions, plus she'll get to hear the background noise, which will provide her with all sorts of information that I'd rather she not know and I'll have to explain a lot more than I want to. She's probably in bed already, lights out, typing her text messages using the built-in blue light of the phone keys, my father sleeping next to her, my mother trying not to wake him because she knows he needs to get a good night's sleep so he can wake by 5:00 and do his rounds at the hospital, because she also knows that if he woke to discover that it is a few minutes past midnight and I am not home yet, he would take the phone out of her hands, demand an explanation as to why I'd decided to breach such a well-established rule like my curfew, especially on a night when there is school the next day and especially so close to finals, when I should be studying, not cavorting, and by then, he would be out of bed, pacing, not shouting because my father never shouts, but certainly and unequivocally *making it very clear*, as in *I want to make this very clear*, that although my life would be spared, there being divine, legal, and moral prohibitions firmly in place against a father killing his daughter (it hasn't happened since the Greeks), the quality of my life would take a decidedly southward plunge, like being inside an elevator in free fall, and even if my father did not wake and my mother did not actually call with an Interrogation, I will, in all likelihood, be grounded—no car, except to go to school and back, no outings with friends for any reason whatsoever (*whatsoever* being one of my mother's favorite words, as *do you understand me?* is one of her favorite phrases with which to conclude the sentencing, closing the door to any appeal).

At this point of the night, the only viable explanation I could offer my parents for having missed my curfew is alien abduction. Not that my parents believe in aliens. (They think the immigration laws in this country are way too lax as they are.) If I can convince them that I was whisked away to the other side of the galaxy, show them the puncture wounds in my lower abdomen, quote verbatim my conversation with Amelia Earhart, I might get them to mitigate the sentence, because being without a car in Miami is the same as being an unperson. You might as well not exist.

Which leads me to the next and last part of this reverie before Michael turns to me and says, "You're coming with us, aren't you?" as everyone has already stood to leave, and I ask, "What about the check?" and reach into my purse for my wallet. Teri turns around to say, "These gentlemen were kind enough to pay for our drinks." And Gloria, who is already twenty feet away, trying to get as close to Alan as she can, loops her arm around his, marking him as her sole property, everyone else KEEP OUT. Right before all this happens and we start our short walk to the beach, down Lincoln Road, toward Washington Avenue, I think about what I'm not supposed to be thinking about, what I promised myself I would drive out of my mind, not "Throbbin' Like an Aneurysm," which thankfully has played its last reprise, but about the last thing I *should* be thinking about, whether Rolly is with Lizette right now and what they are doing. And though thinking about him and Lizette is the last thing I *want* to think about, the thought perversely not only persists but it blooms with details. I make up my mind, I draw an invisible line between then and now, even if the "then" is less than a second ago, about the time it took whatever nerve carried the thought of *then*-ness from wherever thoughts are born to where they are perceived, less time than it takes for me to realize that Michael is standing next to me, looking at me, that he's asked me something. Only when I replay the last few seconds, while the rest of the world went on without me, I hear Michael ask me again, "You're coming with us, aren't you?" and I say, "Yeah," and stand, too quickly, because I upset a glass on the table, fortunately empty, and Michael catches it and sets it upright before it rolls to the edge, and I say, "Sorry," so low that I'm sure he didn't hear me, and he says, "Good thing you didn't have something stronger," and adds, "Sorry," though I've no clue what he's sorry about. And we walk behind the others, sometimes in a group, sometimes dispersing, generally following one direction, Peter next to Teri, talking over his shoulder at Michael and me, Gloria and Alan so far ahead of us that we've almost lost them in the crowd of peddlers, tourists, and troubadours, like the pudgy brown man strumming a big guitar and singing "Bésame mucho," and the small white man strumming a mandolin and yelling "Voe-*lah*-ray, hey!," from one café table to another, people waving both of them away. There's Disco Man dancing to music that's blaring a little too loud for the small speakers in a boom box on the street, dressed like Richard Simmons, with enough enthusiasm to light a small city. "You remember this, don't you?" Disco Man yells. "It's by the beautiful and sexy Donna Summer. Where are you, Donna, when we need you?" Disco Man yells at the sky. The music starts. Tourists point video cameras no bigger than wallets at Disco Man, who takes a few steps forward, claps his hands, spins, and takes a few steps back. I drop money in his box. "Remember Kojak?" Disco Man yells, "Yeah, baby! And the Brady Bunch?"

"You've a truly kind heart," Michael says, after I drop the money.

On Washington Avenue, we walk into a liquor store where Gloria checks her Lotto numbers—nothing—and Teri buys a pack of cigarettes. It's too hot inside, so I stand at the store entrance. A small, hunched-over old man with a long and dirty beard talks emphatically to the empty space in front of him, waves his hands, stabs the air with his index finger. I look at my watch: 12:45 A.M. I look at the sky: no aliens in sight.

"What's he saying?" Alan's standing next to me. I turn.

"Nothing worth translating," Gloria says, taking Alan's arm, pulling him away from me.

Four more blocks, past college students eating slices of pizza so greasy that they lie over their hands like Dalí's clocks, across Collins Avenue, past Ocean Drive, almost peaceful this early Monday morning, an occasional yellow Hummer or black Bentley pumping out beats and long, sustained bass notes that rattle the glass windows, and onto the beach at Fifteenth Street, the glow of the hotels behind us, the flickering pinpoint lights of the ships in the distance, the only sound now that of the palm trees hissing all around us, the dark wind, and our feet landing sharply on the sand.

17. CLOUDS AS BIG AS ISLANDS

The moon's halfway up the sky, big enough to light the sand, the ocean, and the clouds. Teri says something, but nobody answers. When we reach the edge of the ocean, the waves break and glow in the moonlight, before they recede.

Gloria takes off her shoes and walks through the water up to her ankles, running from each wave. Alan follows her closely. She runs into Alan and the wind carries her laughter. They stay close together, two people against the lit and wrinkled surface of the ocean.

At the southernmost tip of the island, a cube on top of a tall building lights, from the bottom up, layer by layer, until it is completely lit. I watch it go through two cycles, when I notice that Teri and Peter have climbed the steps of a lifeguard station and are sitting on the narrow porch.

Michael says, "Shall we stand, or shall we sit?"

We walk away from the water and find a dry spot. I sit, first crossed-legged, then one leg under the other, then my legs straight out. He sits next to me and says that he's been planning this trip all year, that he wants to work somewhere, under the table because he doesn't have that kind of visa.

"Teri's father's a lawyer in a big firm," I say. "Maybe you can go work for them."

"I meant something around here, on the beach. I'm probably going to be stuck breathing recirculated office air for the rest of my working life. Might as well do something different while I can."

"Like what?"

"Like, I don't know, count the number of cigarettes butts on the beach. We're probably sitting on a couple hundred."

"Yuck!" I say, and move, and when I do Michael puts his hand on my arm, and I let him, just like I let him lean over and kiss me.

And it's like walking through a house you've never been in before, kissing Michael. You're taking in the layout, the furniture, what's on the TV, the smells and sounds. I half expect him to grope me, like Rolly would have done, but when he doesn't I relax and let him kiss me some more. And I can tell he's getting excited, but it doesn't matter because I know I'm safe. He can't hurt me. Rolly can't hurt me.

Michael turns and gently pushes me back until I'm lying flat on the sand. There are faint stars in the city-lit sky. A big cloud moves over us, and I imagine that I'm looking at the underside of a large airship. Then it's the stars again. And though Michael's on top of me, I feel none of his weight. *A gentleman always rests his weight on his elbows,* I read somewhere.

Then my phone chirps.

"My mother," I say.

Michael rolls off me, and I rummage through my purse, the inside of which is lit by the phone light flashing blue.

"Where are you? Are you all right? Why aren't you home yet?" It's hard to hear because of the wind. I cup the phone and hope my mother doesn't figure it out.

"I'm going home now," I say.

My mother hangs up.

18. THE LIP OF THE OCEAN

I don't leave, of course. Michael kisses me again, and I lie back on the sand. If I feel his hands undo the buttons of my blouse, I don't stop him. And if I feel his hand on my breast, I let him. I'm thinking, Maybe this is the way it's supposed to happen.

I arch my body because my lower back hurts, and he undoes the button on my jeans. "Wait," I say, and I put my hand over his. "Wait."

Then a woman screams.

"What the fuck!" Michael says, rolling off me.

I snap my bra closed and button my jeans and blouse.

The woman screams again, longer this time. Michael and I run in the direction of her voice. It's Gloria. Alan has his arms around her. Peter and Teri are there too, Teri with her hands against her face. They're standing around what looks like a big trash bag someone's left at the water's edge, except that when we get there, I see it's not a trash bag, but a guy, lying face-down, his jeans pulled down to his ankles, his bare butt and legs gray in this light. The back of his tee shirt reads, I'M A SURFER'S DREAM.

"You think he's alive?" Peter says.

Michael and Alan move to turn the guy face-up.

"Don't touch him," Gloria says.

"Oh, my God!" Teri says.

The boy looks like he's fifteen. His eyes and mouth are closed. His face is drained of all color. Michael and Alan wash their hands in the ocean. Teri says, "Gross!" I look away. There's a thunderstorm in the distance. The clouds light up silently.

19. WHERE WE GO WHEN WE DIE

Michael walks me to my car. On the way, he talks about everything except the dead boy. He asks me about school, about next year, and my plans for college. I tell him what I know, which is that I don't know where I'm going to college or what I'm going to do with the rest of my life. I'm thinking about the boy on the beach, about the police who questioned each of us separately, about their matter-of-factness. My father tells me that life is the exception in a universe that's always on the verge of chaos. He says that the only thing we have is the here and now and our memories of our own past. Other than that, there is nothing. "When we die," he says, "we're dead. Simple as that."

The parking garage elevator is broken, so Michael and I climb the three flights to where my car is parked.

"Nice," he says, patting the car. I offer to drive him back, at least to the corner, a few feet from the café where Alan and Peter will meet him after walking Gloria and Teri to Gloria's car. It's 3:45.

When we reach the corner nearest the café, he asks me for my phone number. He says, "I like you. I know tonight's been rough, but I'm here all summer. And I'd like to see you again."

But before I can answer, my head shakes no. Then I say, "Sorry, but—"

"You don't have to explain," he says. "My loss."

I drive him to the corner of Meridian and Lincoln Road.

"Your friends aren't here yet," I say.

"That's OK. You need to get home." He stops. "OK, then. Thanks for the lift." He opens the door. Then he turns and kisses me on the cheek.

I watch him walk back to the café. Two waiters stack the chairs on the tables and tie them together with a chain and lock.

I haven't driven a block before I regret what I just did. Why didn't I give him my number? Because he's two or three years older than I am, and I'm not ready to date someone that old. Because he's here for the summer, and even if I were ready to date someone that old he'll be gone in a few weeks. Because I don't want to get involved with anyone right now.

I don't want anyone right now.

So this is it, the end of whatever it was I felt for Rolly. It's like discovering you've driven off the road, that sudden rumble of tires scrambling over rocks and dirt and clumps of weeds.

Over the causeway, I look at the city and its lights shining on the bay, against the sky made gray by the clouds lit from below.

I think about the boy.

But all I feel is a blank, like the whiteness of an unmarked page, except it is inside me. I see the boy's tee shirt, his face. The ocean lit by the moon. The thunderstorm in the distance.

It is quiet in the car. Peace.

20. SILVIA

When I get home, my mother's at the front door before I've finished parking the car. She's kinda mad, which I can understand, as it's after 4:00 in the morning. She's not saying anything, but her ears are red. She smells of that cream that she smears all over her face. It's supposed to make you look younger. It has caviar in it and stinks like the sea. Then she starts to talk.

I tell her I'm sorry, but I don't mean it. I should tell her about the dead boy, I think, but then decide against it. I'm sure it'll be on the news. And she doesn't have to know we were there or that we were the ones who found him.

I stop at the door to my room. She looks like she wants to come in, but I block her way.

"OK," she says, "we'll talk later this morning."

And she kisses me good night. I smell my mother's cream and think of the boy.

It takes me a long time to fall asleep. All I can think about is what happened on the beach.

When I finally fall asleep, I don't have a nightmare, as I expect. I don't know if this happens to you, but I have a repertoire of dreams, good ones and bad. There's one where I'm in class taking a quiz that I haven't prepared for. There's another where I'm being chased by someone I cannot see, and all the streetlights are out so everything is dark.

Instead, I have one of my favorite dreams. I'm on a beach on an island. In the distance, there's a rocky cliff that goes right into the water, a straight drop. There's no one else on the island. There's the horizon, the ocean, the waves making the sand tremble under my bare feet, the unmoving cliff. I'm not thinking of anything. I'm not happy or sad or hungry. I miss no one. I just am.

21. METAMORPHOSIS

The next morning, I catch a glimpse of my ex-boyfriend when he speeds down the school's main drive and turns into the new student parking lot. The lot's not paved yet, so his tires kick up a cloud of dust when he puts his brakes on. His windows are up. They buzz with each bass note of whatever music he's playing really loud.

Can anyone really change that much in a few days? Trip Perez on Channel 8 showed a boy who was struck by lightning while waiting for a bus. Not only did the boy survive, he started to levitate. He went from average kid to an inexplicable phenomenon in less than a month. Could Rolly have undergone a similar metamorphosis, from nerd to jerk, in a matter of days? Did Lizette have that much sway over him? More specifically, can having sex change people that much?

Teri and Gloria tell everyone about the boy on the beach, so the rumor gets around the school that we were out on the beach, making out with some foreign guys we'd just met. That's not exactly the kind of rumor I want to get around, but I can't stop it. There's nothing on the radio or the Net about the boy we found dead on the beach. It begins to feel as if I dreamt it up, as if it never happened.

Later that day, I'm standing in line to pay for my lunch in the cafeteria when I see Rolly. He's working his way past people, telling them that he's with me.

"Hey," he says.

I ignore him.

"Got your message."

The cashier tells me what my lunch costs. I open my purse and pay her.

"You're mad, I guess," Rolly says.

The cashier gives me some change. She lays the bills on my palm, then puts the coins on top of the bills, which means that I have to use both hands to take the money. (Can't someone teach these people how to return change? I think irritably.) I put away the money and look for a table. The spaces I see are all next to people I don't know or people I do know but don't want to sit next to.

"I wouldn't blame you if you're mad. Really, I wouldn't. It would be perfectly natural for you to be mad. In fact, it would probably be *un*natural if you weren't."

I'm walking toward the tables. Rolly's behind me, but I don't look back.

"I wanted to say—"

"Rolly, I know what you want to say," I turn, holding the lunch tray between us.

"You do?"

"I know *exactly* what you want to say. There's no need for you to say it."

"But you *are* mad?"

"I'm not mad. Right now, I'm hungry, which is why I'm holding this tray of food. And I'm looking for a place to sit and eat my lunch."

"That's a good idea. Let's sit and talk."

"No. *I* will sit and eat. After that, I'll go to the library until the end of the period and start studying for finals."

Rolly looks at me, at my food, then away. I look out the large windows, down the straight, wide road lined with royal palms, and the light-speckled bay at the end of the road, the water never blinking twice in the same place.

22. NEWTON'S THIRD LAW

Monday night at dinner, my father lectures me about responsibility, consideration, discipline, sexual predators, STDs, white slavery, and the failed British policies in the Middle East. My mother brings the conversation back: no car, except to go to school; no going out for two weeks. "Counted after your last final," my father adds, which means almost one month under this new regime. "Everything has consequences," my mother says. My father nods. No one says anything for a long time.

After dinner, I watch all the local news shows and surf the Internet again. Nothing about the boy.

23. CODA

The rest of the week, I spend most of my time in the library, digging up quotes and stuff I can put into footnotes to pepper my essay for Mrs. Eden. The more footnotes you put in an essay, the more authoritative whatever you write looks. I also page through my vocabulary exercise book and change a few words. "Tiny" becomes "diminutive." "Showoff" turns into "exhibitionist." Mrs. Eden likes it when you use big words.

Monday, a rumor gets around that Mr. Pennington's moved in with Ms. Rodriguez and he's divorcing his wife. I'll believe that when I see it. Another rumor spreads that the parents of a freshman took him out of the school after an incident involving some inappropriate touching perpetrated by one of the social science teachers. The police show up midway through the week and question the teacher, which lends some weight to that story. People say that the boy's parents will sue the school for, like, millions of dollars and that'll kill any plans to build a new gym next year. Others say that the nuns have a lot more money than anyone imagines and the gym will be built as planned, even if they have to pay off the parents.

Tuesday, Rudy Menocal asks me out. I've never liked Rudy. He's not very mature, always yukking it up in class, but I'm grounded anyway, so the point is, as they say in Debating Club, moot.

Wednesday, Gloria tells me that Teri's seeing a shrink. "She's a little freaked about finding the dead boy." My stomach drops. I ask her if it's my father she's seeing, but Gloria says no, the shrink's name is weird. Then she tells me that she exchanged phone numbers with Alan.

"No way. You did that?" I ask her.

She nods, like she's really proud of herself. And I feel something open up inside me. I might see Michael again.

"Why? You interested?"

Even as I shake my head, I start thinking what I would say to Michael when I finally get the nerve to call him. One more thing on my to-do list.

What else happened?

Wednesday night, my parents announce that we're all going on a cruise to the Caribbean. And that I do not have a choice to opt out. I add up the days. The cruise plus the time I'll be grounded eat up half the summer. A cruise is, like, the last thing I want to do, worse than seeing my gynecologist.

My mother also announces that she's starting a diet. The cruise is all she talks about at dinner. Attempts to change the subject by my father or by me are unsuccessful.

What else? Sister Edna catches Richard Gagliano and Karen Mestre doing it in the Moon Temple on Thursday, the next to last day of class. Talk about a dumb move. Both are expelled. The nuns press charges against Richard after he confesses that he's been the one keying the nuns' van, scratching quotations from the Gospels. So the police come for a second time in one week. The word is that the Moon Temple's going to be razed by bulldozers over the summer.

And one more thing. Turns out Rolly and Lizette stopped seeing each other less than a week after they started. Lizette's telling everyone that she dumped Rolly because he was *bor*-ing and a waste in bed. I feel bad for Rolly, but everybody knows the kind of girl she is. He should have known what was coming.

Also on Thursday, for the first time since we broke up, Rolly texts me, starting with the reasonably plaintive lets talk? and the undeniably mature-sounding try to understand me to the feisty its ALL about U!!!! tempered by the irresistibly cute LUV U ♥♥!!!

I don't answer.

On Friday, the last day of class, Mrs. Eden has the five of us read our essays. While I wait my turn, I think about next year. That's the year I'm supposed to pick a college. It's the year I'm also supposed to have a general idea what I want to do with my life. It doesn't have to be specific. I assume I'll be married some day. Maybe I'll have children. I hope I'll fall in love. I pray that I'll meet someone who will love me. Everything else is kinda extra stuff.

Gloria's going to Europe with her parents for the summer. Teri and Francesca are taking a couple of courses at the university for college credit. We're all prepping for the entrance exams.

The fourth student reads her essay, meaning I'm next. I work on my list of things I need to do next year. I write "I'm a surfer's dream" in the margins and cross it out.

When Mrs. Eden calls my name and reads the title of my essay, the boys whoop and howl. "Children," Mrs. Eden says. "Yes, I said 'children' because you are acting like people half your age." That only encourages the boys to whoop louder.

I read my essay and concentrate on the paper. I try not to think about anything that's happened in the last two weeks, not even about the boy on the beach. Every so often, someone makes a rude remark like, "Is this from experience you're talking, Silvia?" And Mrs. Eden points her finger at the offender, once interrupting me to say, "Don't think it's too late for me to hand out a little extra homework, young man. I'm sorry, Silvia. Go ahead." I don't look up because I don't want to lose my place. By the second page, the class is quiet. By the third, I'm thinking only of the words that I hear myself say. By the fourth page, the paper has become transparent.

When I'm finished, there is a second of silence. Then polite applause. Mrs. Eden is standing. She's motioning to the class to applaud louder. More whoops. More howls. I keep my eyes on the floor.

After class, Gloria, Teri, and some of the other girls congratulate me. Someone taps my shoulder. Mariella Poza is standing behind me.

"You seem interesting," she says, folding a stick of gum into her mouth. "Next year, remind me to talk to you."

I add Mariella's name to the list of things I have to do.

The Last Flight
of José Luis Balboa

PETE BURGER

I've never cheated on Cheryl. She and I have been dating for five years. I think it's stupid to say that you're dating when you're both over thirty. Cheryl tells people that we're dating and going steady. I cringe when she says shit like that.

I've never even thought about cheating on her. But now I'm on South Beach, sitting on the sand near two beautiful girls who are lying with their tops off, and I've been thinking about nothing else. Not that I would ever do anything.

One girl sits up to turn over and lie on her stomach. When she does so, her blondish hair falls forward into her face. She uses both hands to pull her hair back and tie it, giving me a view of her breasts, which are tanned and full. And though I don't want to, I can't help but think how pale Cheryl's breasts are. I know I shouldn't, but that's just what pops into my head.

The blondish girl's done with her hair. She catches me looking at her breasts but instead of making a face or a snide remark, she smiles at me. Then she rests her chin on the towel and closes her eyes. I look at her, hoping to get her attention, but she keeps her eyes closed. Her back is smooth and tanned too.

The other girl has short black hair and wraparound sunglasses. Her breasts don't look as pretty, but I won't be able to tell for sure until she sits up because right now they're just lying flat against her chest. I can see her hipbones.

There's no way I'm going to take off my shirt even though it feels as if it's about to melt onto the skin on my back.

I'm on my third beer. It's getting warm and it tastes bitter, but I drink it anyway. I think about Cheryl and feel a little guilty for what I was thinking earlier, about the breasts, I mean. I wish I could delete the guilt, uninstall it like a program. Problem solved. Everything runs faster.

Forget the girls. I think of the sun lighting up half the planet, from Prague to Honolulu, and it makes me feel expansive. I look out to sea, past the waves breaking on the beach and the dark heads of the bathers and strips of green water lit by the sun, past the WaveRunners and the small boats and even the large cargo ships on the horizon, gray cutouts doing nothing. And I try to picture what's on the other side of the horizon. Is it Africa?

Africa's where my brother, Tom, lives.

The blondish girl asks me if I have the time. I nod and look at my watch. She taps her friend on the shoulder and says something in Spanish. Her friend laughs but she doesn't look.

"How complicated," the blondish girl says, pointing at my watch. What the hell, I think. I show her all the features—the twenty-four time zones, the five alarms, stopwatch, countdown watch—speaking over the sound of the wind and the waves. When I look at her, I focus on the spot between her eyebrows.

Now the other girl turns around and rests her chin in her hands. She's smiling. I'm encouraged, so I keep talking about the watch. Then I introduce myself.

The blondish girl says her name is Maylin. I hear Marilyn, but she corrects me. I have trouble understanding her. The accent, I guess. The dark-haired girl says her name is Jasmine and shakes my hand. Then Maylin does the same, soft, ladylike. Where I come from, girls never shake your hand.

Maylin, Jasmine. I try to make a joke, emphasizing the rhyme in the second syllables of their names, but they look at me as if I've just rattled off random numbers.

I'm feeling self-conscious. My underarms smell, and I run my hand over my face.

Girls like Maylin and Jasmine usually look right through me. After years of working in windowless rooms with fluorescent lights, living on Coke and pizza, it's obvious that I'm not from here. Everyone else is practically naked.

The company flew me down to troubleshoot a program. Nothing major. It's happened before with this version of the software. All I had to do was take the system offline, install the patch, and reboot. That simple. Even running the diagnostics, the whole thing took me less than four hours. So I'm left with the entire day to lie on the beach, drink some of this Presidente beer, and enjoy the view. I could have caught a plane home this morning, but any change to my itinerary would have come out of my pocket. Plus Cheryl's been in a bitch of a mood since Thanksgiving when her younger sister announced that she's pregnant. For three never-ending days her mother asked us mercilessly, *How about you? What are you waiting for? You two ever going to get married?* Each time she did, I felt blood rush to my face and an almost irresistible impulse to set her house on fire. She made Cheryl cry. Her father was more diplomatic. He said people who don't have children are self-centered and immature. Tom's a priest in Nigeria helping people with AIDS. He doesn't have children, so I guess he's what Cheryl's father would call self-centered and immature.

My own parents warned me not to lead Cheryl on. They told me to marry the girl or let her be, as if I kept her chained in a dungeon, with nothing to eat but bread and water. *When I was your age,* my father e-mailed me around New Year's, *your mom and I were married, we had Tom, and I bought our first house.* That was my father's way of telling me, in twenty words, that he wants me to get married, have a family, and buy my own place. My father thinks people who rent are suspect.

One Sunday morning in January, Cheryl was making coffee in the kitchen. I shuffled in and was about to say something when she told me that marriage and babies were off-limits. We were not to talk about those two subjects. OK, I said, unconvinced that I had given up anything before I watched her finish pouring water into the top of the coffee machine. Peace and quiet fell over us like nightfall in a valley, until last Saturday. On my way to her place, I called her to ask if she needed anything from the supermarket. Cheryl said she'd expected to have a baby by now. The statement, a non sequitur, apropos of absolutely nothing, made me wonder if my cell phone had picked up a stray signal. I repeated the question, more slowly this time. She'd expected to be someone's wife, a mother by now, she said louder. I pretended to lose the call. Hello? Hello? I said. Like I really needed that shit.

So why take an earlier flight and hurry home when I can sit here, talk with Maylin and Jasmine, and enjoy a beer and the view? There's an ultralight buzzing overhead. It has wings that are different shades of yellow.

I catch Maylin looking at me.

"Kay *pah*-zah?" I say.

Maylin covers her mouth and laughs. I point at the ultralight. And either she really doesn't know what I'm talking about or she's pretending. Then she comes over to where I'm sitting, crouches down behind me, places both her hands on my shoulders, and looks down my arm to where I'm pointing. I can feel her breath on the back of my neck. She says something in Spanish, but I understand about eight words in that language, and I've used up two of them already. Anyway, I'm not thinking about the damn ultralight anymore.

RICHARD JOLICOEUR, PH.D.

I'm driving my taxi from South Beach to downtown. In the back are two Americans. They are dressed in dark suits and carry briefcases. One of them speaks a little Spanish and addresses me in that language. He asks me to turn off the music. I am playing Beethoven's *Pastorale* from a set of CDs of Herbert von Karajan conducting the Berlin Philharmonic. I wasn't even playing it very loud.

"I prefer silence too," I tell him in English. "The music is for the benefit of my passengers. If they do not like it, I turn it off. I want all my passengers to relax and enjoy Miami," I say. "I am from Haiti," I say, but the Americans say nothing. Occasionally, a passenger notices the "Ph.D." after my name, which I wrote in a thick black marker on my cabdriver's license. Then I'm asked what kind of doctor and why I left Haiti and so on. I watch the two men in the rearview mirror. They seem distracted, looking out their windows. So I decide to take the scenic route. We'll go down Ocean Drive, right on Fifth, across the bay on the causeway so I can point out Fisher Island and the other island, where Gloria Estefan lives. On Watson Island, they can see the cruise ships and the buildings downtown across the bay. It is my favorite view of Miami. On days when business is slow I'll park my cab to watch the sun set. At night it is especially beautiful. After the causeway, I'll turn south on Biscayne Boulevard, point out the Arena, the Freedom Tower, Bayside, then turn into downtown. My best fares are tourists who want me to show them the sights. A fare like that can make me fifty to one hundred dollars because I'll take them all over—the Design District, the Grove, the Gables. "We have so many beautiful things to see in Miami," I tell the Americans in the back, but they do not respond. Their heads are down. I hear them shuffling papers.

We are stopped at a red light on Ocean Drive. Young girls in tangas on their way to the beach cross in front of my taxi. The Americans do not look up. Maybe they like men. I try to not judge.

MARÍA ISABEL COSTA

With a pair of scissors, I cut the line to the phone in the study, cut the line to the phone in the bedroom and the phone in the living room. Then I take the answering machine, open the sliding glass doors, and throw it over the balcony. I throw out the cell phones too. What else? I cut the TV cable and the computer cable and the whole spaghetti mess of wires behind his stereo.

I open his closet and tear his shirts and pants. The suits are too hard, so I stuff them into paper bags and drop the bags down the trash chute in the hall.

I return to the kitchen and pour myself more champagne. The phones started ringing a few minutes after he left. It was as if he'd tipped off the press. TV people, newspaper people, friends, friends of friends called, all wanting me to confirm what they already knew —that José Luis is leaving me.

My producer was the last to call. He wanted to know if I would be able to make the taping tomorrow. *Oh, Mari, I am so sorry about José Luis. You must be devastated,* he said. But I knew the real reason he called. *I know this is a difficult time for you, but I wanted to know.* "If I am going to make it in tomorrow? Yes, Sammy. I will be there tomorrow. And the next day. And the day after that!" That's when I slammed the phone down so hard that I cracked the glass table underneath.

At least if I had had the baby, then there would be something of José Luis left for me. But he insisted that I get an abortion. And even if I can barely remember the clinic and that nurse who reminded me of the nuns at school, there was the pain. First physical. Then nothing. Less than nothing. A negative that drew me in, made me want to explore it, like you do a broken tooth with the tip of your tongue. It hurts each time you touch it, but you cannot stop. Then the memory yellows. And only enough of the old pain remains so that you do not forget. There are venial sins and cardinal sins and mortal sins, the kind of sins you can never erase. Like India ink. They stain your soul forever. My soul must look like a smoker's lungs.

PETE BURGER

Maylin and Jasmine speak English. They were just pretending not to understand me. I laugh along. OK, I'm a little annoyed. But I drink some more beer and imagine everything being sucked through a black hole into another universe—Cheryl, her parents, my father's e-mails.

Maylin tells me that she's from Colombia. She's here to study English. I tell her where I'm from. She nods as if she's heard of it. Jasmine, she says, is her cousin. She's visiting for the summer. Maylin's family has a condo. Her father heads the Colombian branch of an American multinational. The name of the company sounds familiar. Jasmine makes a joke about the condo, but Maylin elbows her to be quiet. Maylin says her brother lives with her. He's training to be a pilot. Her parents want him to look after her, but he's too busy with his studies and his American girlfriend. So Jasmine's here for the summer to keep her company.

"Don't you have a boyfriend?" I ask her.

Maylin shakes her head. Jasmine nods.

More games, I think.

They ask me what I do, and I tell them almost everything. I leave Cheryl out. No need to complicate things. I tell them about my work and where I'm staying. They're impressed. I shrug my shoulders, but I'm glad. Now we're getting somewhere.

So we're talking, having a nice time. Jasmine puts her top on and says she's going to buy drinks from the kiosk nearby. I dig in my pocket to give her cash, but she waves my hand away. I watch her run over the hot sand. I am fascinated by the physics of her bathing suit.

Something catches Maylin's attention, and I turn to look. Two guys wearing sleeveless tee shirts and long gym pants come toward us. They are muscular. One has shaved his head. The other has long hair in a ponytail. The one with the shaved head crouches down and talks to Maylin in Spanish, and I'm thinking it's her brother or a boyfriend. Ponytail stands behind me. Maylin's saying something. She points to me. Then the guy looks at me and smiles.

"Hi, roe," he says. Or hi-lo. I can't really tell. He offers his hand, which is twice the size of mine.

I tell him my first name. I'm trying my best to be friendly, show him that I don't want trouble. He says that he hopes everything is OK. And as he says this, he holds up one hand and joins the tips of his index finger and thumb, forming a circle. Then he pushes his other index finger back and forth through the circle and waits for me to react. When I don't, he laughs and stands and says bye-bye. Maylin moves her own index finger in circles next to her head and says something that sounds like "low-coe," which I know means crazy in Spanish. I turn to look for the other guy, but he's walking away, next to Hi-Lo.

MARÍA ISABEL COSTA

I close all the curtains. I do not want to see the sky or the ocean. I do not want to see José Luis flying that stupid contraption of his as if this were any Sunday, as if we had not made love last night and early this morning and he had not held me, before we got up to have breakfast and he became serious and quiet. When I asked him about it, he didn't want to say anything. Not at first. Until I insisted, and he told me that it was over, only this time it is for good, Isabel. He denied there was anyone else. But I knew. How could I not know? *Hola* printed a picture of him snuggling with that model, the one with the funny name that sounds like an Austrian pastry. I can't even say it. What kind of a name is that? And she, a head taller than him. They look ridiculous together.

How could he have been so calm last night and pretended that everything was fine?

Last night, we ate at Sushi Pazzo. People came to our table. José Luis stood to shake their hands. One of our friends said how happy we looked. After dinner, he ordered the driver to drop us a few blocks from our apartment so we could walk along the beach.

The ocean looked phosphorescent when the waves broke on the sand. We took off our shoes and watched our feet disappear in the foamy water. José Luis held my hand and we walked the rest of the way in silence. And I thought that whatever had happened between him and that model was over. At home, he made love to me more tenderly than usual. How could I have known?

I get another bottle of champagne out of the refrigerator and open it, steadying it as I pour the wine into the glass.

This morning too, he was tender. Unless I am on assignment or José Luis is on tour, on Sundays we sleep late and eat breakfast together. The maid takes the day off, so we have the condo to ourselves.

José Luis made love to me again and held me for a long time. It wasn't until breakfast that his mood changed and he was quiet.

When he finished eating, he said, "We have been together almost four years. Plenty of time, I think, for us to know whether this will work."

Something sour sprang up into my mouth, but I ignored it and ate another piece of melon.

"Don't think that I am not grateful," he said, "or that I have forgotten everything you did for me. I will never forget that." He reached for my hand. I drew it back.

Three months after we met, I realized that I was in love with José Luis, and I asked him to move into my apartment. At that time, I was the one making all the money. José Luis was living with that useless poet he thinks so highly of, sleeping on the couch of a studio apartment near Eighth Street. That was almost a year before he became famous and rich with his song "Isabel," which he wrote for me, which he could not have written without me. Back then, he drank a bottle of vodka every day or else he could not write, he said, or else the world was such a sharp-edged place that he hurt just being in it and he could not feel the music inside him. The alcohol dulled the world, he said. It protected him from all the sharpness. So he drank.

I had not noticed it before he moved in, but so many things do not become evident until you live with someone. Every few days, he drank until he could not stand. When he threw up on me in bed while we slept, I told him that was enough and forced him to enter a clinic. The doctor said he could have drowned in his own vomit. He could have died had it not been for me.

You owe me your miserable life, you bastard, I thought.

José Luis looked at his plate.

"Just say it," I said. "It should be easy for you."

"This time it is for good, Isabel. I'm leaving and I'm not coming back."

He gave me a little speech. He had obviously prepared it, maybe even with the help of his model friend, Miss Austrian Pastry. It was his thank-you speech to me, like the one he delivered last year when he won a Latin Grammy for "Isabel." He thanked his producer, his agent, all his friends. Thank you, thank you.

"You will always be very special to me," he said.

I slapped him. Hard. Something rose inside me and I slapped him again. And when he dropped his face into his hands, I took a deep breath and hit his ears, the back of his neck. I stood, balled up my fists, and pounded him on his back, his head, frustrated that my blows did not seem to hurt him, not wanting to hurt him, angry at my impotence.

He wrapped his arms around my legs and picked me up and carried me to the living room. I cried, but I kept hitting him. He put me down on the sofa, stepped back, and watched me try to catch my breath between sobs.

When he came closer I kicked at him, but he grabbed my legs by the ankles and held them.

"Are you going to rape me too?" I screamed.

He stopped, let go of my legs, and backed away.

RICHARD JOLICOEUR, PH.D.

We are at another red light on Ocean Drive, in front of the house where Gianni Versace was shot. Three girls and a young man embrace and smile on the steps where Versace died while another woman takes their picture. I look away, toward the ocean, and see a glider going up and down and around. The way it moves reminds me of a fly buzzing about food. I have never seen anything like that. I even say "Hey, look!" to the Americans in the back, and they look up from their papers. One of them says, "It's an ultralight."

"Look at the way it is flying," I say. And I feel there is going to be trouble even though I do not want to believe it. I feel the nothingness swell within me. I hope my passengers do not notice.

When I was a child, my mother told me that I could sense the future. My spinster aunt visited us, hoping that I would help her find a man. We sat at the kitchen table, my mother at one end, my aunt at the other. My aunt asked me to tell her if this or that man was a good match. When I told her that I did not sense anything, my mother took my hand, put it on my aunt's forehead, and told me to try harder, concentrate. My aunt never married. She died a year later of a rare disease. That confirmed my powers to my mother. "Of course you sensed nothing. What you sensed was death," she said, blessing herself.

As a teenager, I rebelled and stopped believing in God and all the saints. I studied philosophy and worshiped Progress and Science. It was religion, voodoo, dictators, and coups d'état that kept my country poor, hungry, and ignorant. I wanted to leave all that behind.

Once I started university in Port-au-Prince, I spoke only French, even when I telephoned back home. I saved money and bought a pipe that I carried unlit because I could not afford to buy good tobacco and was not about to smoke the black, foul-smelling stuff that our washerwoman smoked. My mother made fun of me and called me *monsieur le professeur.* I won a scholarship to study in Paris. I pretended that I was French and modern, but if I had sounded very French in Haiti, now I sounded very Haitian in France. The other students wanted to talk about the things I was most embarrassed to discuss. Can you put a spell on people? they asked me. Can you make me go into a trance? Sometimes I gave in, touched their foreheads, and told them what I saw. I had left Haiti to become someone else, but the truth was that I had brought my country with me.

When I was awarded my *doctorat,* I returned to Haiti. I had my little library of philosophy books and my stylish French clothes. I tried to adapt to life in Port-au-Prince, but my country has no need for people like me. It wants only soldiers or politicians or merchants, and I am none of those. So I left again. This time for Miami. I packed my *doctorat,* some clothes, and all my books. I had no clue what I would do. Maybe I would teach at a university, some place like Texas or Oklahoma, some quiet American place. But the closest I came to teaching was when a private school in Miami interviewed me for a position as assistant librarian. I even took a typing test. They said they would call me back, but they never did. That was thirteen years ago. Since then at home there has been more unrest, more poverty. I have never returned.

I ask my mother to come here. Each time she gives me the same answer. She cannot leave Haiti because my sister and her children are there, because who would look after the house, *your* house after I die, she says, because my father is buried not ten minutes away. So many becauses.

My sister and her husband have a good business. They import electrical appliances from Miami. I see my brother-in-law several times a year. Last year, he brought my sister and their two children. Haiti is good to men like him. He sells you practical things that make your life easier.

The traffic light changes to green. I drive slowly, trying not to lose sight of the glider, which is now diving and climbing again.

PETE BURGER

Jasmine returns with a couple of beers for me and two bottles of water for herself and Maylin. I hold out some money to pay for my beers, but she puts her hand on mine and squeezes it before she pushes it away. She sits facing me. Maylin kneels behind Jasmine to unsnap the top of her bathing suit. Jasmine says that her breasts are too white. She cups them in her hands and looks at me. I tell her they're fine and take a drink. Fine? she says, cocking her head. *Bway*-noe, I say. *Rico*, Maylin says, and smacks her lips. They both laugh. Maylin gives Jasmine the bottle of suntan oil before she lies down on her back. Jasmine squeezes a line of oil across her breasts. Using both hands she spreads the oil evenly. Then she turns and lies next to Maylin.

I watch them. I want to remember this, regardless of what happens. It will be something I will never tell anyone, something I can call up when I'm waiting for a program to download and I'm bored. I want to take it all in, turn myself into a camera. More than a camera because I want to remember what the breeze feels like and how the music coming from the hotel behind me rises and falls with the wind. When the wind shifts, you can hear the steady beat from the pool bar. The wind carries the beat over the low dunes capped with sea oats, between wire-mesh trash baskets overflowing with garbage and people carrying beach chairs and coolers. A tractor plows the sand and moves slowly north. The sound of its engine is a steady rumble. The tractor clears a wide swath of sand between the dunes and us. The sand there is hard and compact. A steady stream of joggers and power walkers flow over it wearing headphones, looking straight ahead.

Closer to the water, a small village of blue umbrellas and chaises longues are arranged on the beach into rows. Most of the chaises are occupied by middle-aged couples reading newspapers and paperback books. Two couples nearby are having an animated discussion in French. A dozen young men and women dressed in white shirts and shorts run between the hotel pool bars and the beach carrying trays of drinks and food. Closer still, unprotected by any umbrellas and ignored by the waiters, are the younger people, like Maylin and Jasmine, lying on beach towels and smoking cigarettes. Most of them are talking on their cell phones. Almost all the young women are topless. The boys sit separately. Occasionally, a boy will ask a girl for a cigarette.

Along the edge of the water, men in big bathing shorts and women wearing small bikinis walk south and north, looking at the sights. There are no children.

Heads and shoulders bob in the shallow green water. Three Jet Skis buzz behind them. A man swims toward a sandbar.

Beyond that, three motorboats have dropped anchor. A man dives off the deck of one boat. Two women lie on the deck of another. On the horizon, too far to make out any details, are the unmoved gray ships.

The ultralight flies low over the water.

Jasmine and Maylin lie next to each other. Jasmine's hand finds Maylin's and caresses it.

Maybe I should leave, I think. I'm not hungry, but I could eat. I could sleep too. Besides, what do I think I'm doing here? It isn't as if I'm going to do anything with these two. I've had my fun.

Cheryl's a nice woman. She loves me. OK, so the passion's gone. Sex is something we do, like getting a haircut or washing the car. But sex isn't everything. Someday, we'll get married. I'm not keen on children, but they're kind of a package deal with Cheryl, and if that's what she wants, then I'll do it. Won't be the end of the world. Plenty of people have children. You go to the mall and all you see are children. There's no getting around it, having children is part of life, like jerking off, squeezing pimples, growing your hair long, then losing it, voting Democrat, before you grow up and vote Republican (that's what my father says).

Enough, I think. I've probably drunk too much beer. On an empty stomach, in this heat, no wonder it went straight to my head.

I lie back on the sand and close my eyes and let the ocean breeze flow over me. And I wonder whether the air carries some bit of Africa, maybe a grain of sand, something of the land where my brother lives.

I love my brother. He found a purpose for his life. I have mostly stumbled through mine. In college, I changed majors so often that it took me six years to finish, and when I did it was with the lowest average you could get and still graduate. I took a job as a computer tech in a law firm. I told myself that I'd do that for a little while before I'd do something else, something that mattered. From the law firm, I went to work at an insurance company. From there, I went to a payroll company. And from there, I came to my current job. I've been at it four years. Sometimes I think it's stupid to look for a purpose to life. It's like asking why the sky is blue or why the sun rises in the east. There's a scientific reason for it, but there's no why, not in the big sense.

I sit up. The tractor is coming back. I watch it make neat straight grooves, like the kind you see in a Japanese garden, grooves that are supposed to make you feel peace and balance. A thin man walks two black Labradors along the water. The dogs run in and out of the water and shake themselves dry. Three girls walking the opposite way stop and try to pet the dogs. The man smiles patiently, but it is obvious that he wants to walk on.

The beer is too hot to drink so I empty the bottle and bury it. I dig my fingers into the hard sand. A shard of seashell stabs one of my nail beds. It hurts, but I do not move my finger. The pain makes me feel more alive.

Maylin is lying on her stomach, looking at me. One hand lies on Jasmine. The other is under her chin. Her fingers caress her lips. Watching her unsettles me. I want her. I want Jasmine too.

The sun has started to drop behind me. The sky is a deeper blue. The clouds look like they glow from within.

The ultralight comes around and climbs again, more steeply this time.

MARÍA ISABEL COSTA

I jumped on him. He fell back. We rolled on the Persian rug. He pushed me off so hard that my head hit the edge of the coffee table. I must have lost consciousness because when I opened my eyes again I was lying down.

He pressed a cool towel to my cheeks and my head. I told him that it stung.

"I think you broke the skin."

He said he would get some ice and left. Maybe it is a good thing that he goes, I thought. Maybe we are too passionate, and if we stay together we will kill each other.

I heard him move about in the kitchen, open the freezer, close it.

Maybe he will kill himself. Or I will. Passions this strong always find a way to express themselves. They have their own imperatives.

Like when he crashed his ultralight into the ocean last year. I was on a chaise longue on the beach, under an umbrella, reading a paperback novel. I read a page, then put it down to watch José Luis take off. A slip of paper marks the page I was reading when it happened, when I heard a man yell, Check it out! I looked up in time to see the crash. It was so quiet that if it hadn't been for the man yelling, I would never have seen a thing.

I took care of José Luis while he was in the hospital. At home, I handed him the pills that the doctors gave him for the pain. He swallowed them with cognac, even though his doctor told him to avoid alcohol.

When he could walk again, when he was ready to go back to work, he came up behind me and embraced me, whispering in my ear how much he loved me, how much he appreciated that I had cared for him. He kissed me.

"You could have killed yourself," I told him.

Not long after that, he bought another ultralight. He flies it on Sunday afternoons, after our late breakfasts, after we make love and go back to sleep and lie in bed talking. I do not go to the beach with him anymore. I know he will crash again and I do not want to see it when it happens. Instead, I lie on the sofa in the living room and read or watch movies. I like old American movies from the forties. The characters seem so mature, so different from today. Someone will tell me when he crashes, I'm sure.

He came back from the kitchen with a bag of ice. "Try to sleep," he said, putting the bag against my head.

"Where are you going?"

"You're not hurt badly. Just the skin. That's all. You're OK."

"I think I scratched you, on your cheek."

"It's nothing."

He went to the study and closed the door. He talked on the phone. I could hear his muffled voice. I could have walked over and listened, but I did not want to. I didn't want anything, just to lie in the dark and quiet, to close my eyes. It wasn't that I didn't care. To say that you do not care is itself a declaration of some feeling.

When he returned, he faced away from me as he changed and dressed for the beach.

"Where are you going? You can't—after everything that happened today."

"Why not?"

"Because—"

"Nothing has changed, Isabel. I go flying on Sundays, you know that."

"Don't you care about me?"

"I do," he said, standing in his closet on the other side of the room. "But nothing has changed. I'll move out this week."

He finished dressing. I turned my head away when he leaned over to kiss me. Then he left.

That's when the phone started to ring. I would have ignored it, except that the caller hung up every time the answering machine came on and called again. After the fourth time, I picked up the phone next to the bed.

Everyone knew that José Luis was leaving me. Reporters from TV, magazines and newspapers, friends, associates from the talk show. Even my competitor called to stick the knife in deeper. "Do you know that she made over fifteen million dollars modeling last year?" she told me about Miss Austrian Pastry. I slammed down the phone and disconnected myself from the rest of the world. I did not want the rest of the world anymore. All my life I wanted to project myself into hundreds of thousands of TV screens, into the minds of millions of people. My show is still the best and most watched. I've worked very hard and done what no other woman on Spanish-language TV has done. I've opened doors. Now I want quiet. And dark. Nothing.

I take the glass and the bottle with me and walk carefully out of the kitchen, into the long hall that leads to the main bathroom, and put the bottle and the glass on the marble top, so I can open the medicine chest. I see the pills that the doctor gave José Luis when he crashed his ultralight, the ones that he mixed with cognac because he said that otherwise they did not work. And I think that if he wants to kill himself that's his problem. He already crashed once. People like that do not learn. They do not care about the pain they cause others. It has always been about him.

RICHARD JOLICOEUR, PH.D.

The driver behind me blows his horn. I speed up, keeping my eye on the beach. When I catch sight of the glider again, it is stuck in the sky. For a second, it doesn't move. Then it falls straight into the ocean.

"Did you see that?" I yell and slow down. The driver behind me blows his horn, and the American who speaks Spanish says that they have an appointment downtown, that they would appreciate it if I would please take the quickest and most direct route. Then he says something to the other one, and he laughs. I can't hear what he said, but I don't like the sound of it.

PETE BURGER

The thin man with the Labradors is talking to the girls when the ultralight crashes silently into the water. The dogs bark, but the man does not look and neither do the girls.

MARÍA ISABEL COSTA

I try to stand, but I cannot. Maybe I took too many pills. I shook them into my palm and did not count them. Then there were so few left in the bottle that I swallowed the rest.

I want some more champagne, but my wrists feel as if they are ringed by weights. With my fingers I find the remote control and rewind the tape on the VCR. I am watching a concert José Luis gave a year ago. I am watching him sing "Isabel."

"But María's too common a name," he told me the first time we went out. He took me to Costa Brava, and we sat on the second floor so we could be the center of attention. I met Enrique Iglesias, who was sitting at a table on the other side of the room. José Luis walked over there to say hello and waved for me to join them.

"What's your middle name?" José Luis asked me after dinner on the way home.

"Isabel," I say to the stilled image of José Luis bringing his mouth close to the microphone.

Two weeks after that dinner, he played the song for me. We were at the poet's apartment. He told me that it had been a difficult song to write, that it had tested him as an artist. "How do you capture beauty?" he said. I blushed and started to say thank you, but he put his finger on my lips. Then he played the song. "Isabel."

RICHARD JOLICOEUR, PH.D.

My head snaps forward, then back against the headrest when I hit the brakes harder than I expected. The driver behind me blows his horn angrily. I look in the rearview mirror, but my trunk lid is up.

"OK?" I ask the Americans. One of them nods. Out of my side-view mirror, I see the driver behind me getting out of his taxi, so I get out too.

"What is happening?" the American asks me, still in Spanish.

"No problem," I answer him in English.

I know the other driver. His name is Ronny. He is from Cap-Haïtien.

"Ronny," I tell him, "I am sorry." And I point to the glider, which now looks like crumpled paper floating in the ocean. A traffic cop shows up and tries to listen to Ronny and me explain what happened, but the cop waves his hands in the air and tells us to stop, stop, he cannot listen to both of us speaking at once, so he takes my documents, which I have ready to show him how cooperative I am, and he pulls Ronny aside. I look back at the glider. The heads of half a dozen people bob in the water around it. I turn to my cab and see the Americans getting out with their briefcases.

"Wait!" I yell.

"We do not have time," the one who speaks Spanish yells back at me. I am about to say something else, like, This will only take a minute, or tell them that I would cut the fare in half or to a quarter, anything not to lose them, but they are too fast. They wave down another taxi, get in with their briefcases, and drive off.

That is when I feel the traffic cop standing next to me. I tell him about the glider crashing, but all he does is nod as he writes the ticket. "Do you think the pilot is hurt?" I say. The cop ignores me, so I look out at the water. A helicopter is over the glider, flattening the water, sending concentric rings out. The cop hands me the ticket, something to do with my license, and my documents, and tells me to move my car before he arrests me and sends me back to where I belong.

I apologize to the cop. Then I try to close the lid of the trunk, but each time I slam it down, it pops back up. I do this several times. Ronny brings some rope and together we tie the lid shut.

"I am sorry, Ronny. Really I am," I tell him.

"I am sorry too," Ronny says, shaking my hand.

I get into my taxi and drive off. The meter is still ticking. I flip the flag down harder than I should.

I have no place to go. I can return to the hotel, but no one is going to want to ride in a car that looks like this. And I'll have to think of an excuse to tell the cab company. This is my only accident in all the years I have been driving. No one has ever complained about me. The company will be mad, perhaps, but it can't overlook all my years of service.

I take the causeway inland and drive past Fisher Island, past the entrance to the island where Gloria Estefan lives, past the cruise ships, past all the sights I would have shown the two Americans, if they had not run off without paying me. On Watson Island, I turn off the causeway.

PETE BURGER

I overhear that the guy in the ultralight is a celebrity, some Latin singer. Soon after the crash all the TV stations are out on the beach pointing their cameras at the water. But by then the rescue people have taken the guy and the ultralight away, and there's nothing to see except a lot of people dying to get on TV. The word is he's dead meat. Kind of stupid, I think, to die like that.

MARÍA ISABEL COSTA

The video is on pause. Frozen on the screen is a close-up of José Luis's face, his lips almost touching the microphone. I close my eyes. My head drops on the pillow. I do not dream.

PETE BURGER

The funny thing that happens is that while we're watching the coast guard and the police pull the body out of the water, Maylin and Jasmine stand next to me. Each takes an arm and stands close, as if we've known each other forever. Maybe it's part of their culture. I've heard that Latins are affectionate, so I'm fine with it.

Then Maylin lays her cheek against my arm, and Jasmine puts her arm around my waist, and before I know what's coming out of my mouth, I'm inviting these girls to my room.

The beach is still crowded when the girls pick up their things and we walk toward the dunes, holding hands. Jasmine says she's hungry, and Maylin says she wants something to drink. Yeah, like rum and Coke or something, Jasmine says. They know this liquor store that's on the same block as the hotel.

We pass other couples, and I can tell the men and even the women can't believe their eyes when they see me between these two lovelies.

We get a liter bottle of white rum and a liter bottle of Coke and take it back to the room, where Jasmine prepares the drinks. Maylin throws herself on the bed and plays with the stereo on the night table. I'm looking at Maylin when Jasmine hands me a glass. It's a little strong, but I drink it. Why spoil the party?

She hands me another, and I drink that too. Then Jasmine's kissing me, putting her tongue in my mouth.

Maylin says something, so I sit on the bed next to her, and we kiss. I don't know how long we do this because by the time I look again, Maylin's naked, Jasmine has her top off, and I'm stripped to my shorts.

Like I said, I'm a beer guy. Rum's not my drink. I'm starting to feel the room turn. I tell Jasmine this, when she hands me another drink, but as I'm getting the words out she takes my hand and places it over her breast. Then she kisses me some more.

Maylin pulls off my shorts and takes me in her mouth. I'm drunk by then and can't feel a thing.

I don't hear the door open. Maylin and Jasmine pull away. I try to make my mouth form the word "hey" when I'm wrestled to the bed, face-down. My hands and feet are tied. Someone stuffs a rag in my mouth and ties another rag around my face. I can't make a sound.

Ponytail turns me over while Hi-Lo examines me.

"He's a little fat," Ponytail says.

"So what if he's fat?" Hi-Lo says. "So long as he has all his parts, he'll be fine."

Ponytail and Hi-Lo carry a large trunk into the room and place it by the bed. They lift me off the bed and put me in the trunk.

"Aren't you going to throw his clothes in too?" Ponytail says.

"What for? He won't need them."

Then they close the lid.

RICHARD JOLICOEUR, PH.D.

I turn off the air conditioner and open the windows. I drive to the end of the road, to the small parking lot next to the fish market and the docks. The market is closed, but the stand is open. I buy a beer from the surly woman with beefy arms who tends the stand. I drink my beer and look out at the water and the city beyond it, trying to forget about the glider.

I get another beer. The surly woman tells me to make sure I'm not caught driving drunk and nods in the direction of a police car that is parked at the end of the lot. I smile. I like to be polite to everyone. I walk back to my car and drink and watch the sun set, the sky change color, and the buildings light up. The lights shine on the bay, restless yellows, blues, and whites.

I wonder if the pilot of the glider got out all right. It would be a real tragedy to fall out of the sky like that and die. It would make no sense.

I turn on the music, the *Pastorale* from the beginning, and listen to it with my eyes closed. I put things in perspective: I am a taxi driver, not a philosopher or a professor or even an assistant librarian. I am a small-time taxi driver who got into a small-time accident this afternoon and lost a small-time fare because he was distracted by a glider crashing into the water. I should have been paying attention to the road. That is what I am paid to do.

When I open my eyes again, the music has stopped. The surly woman is closing the shutters of the stand. I sit up. The surface of the bay is calm.

Maybe the newspaper will say something about the glider tomorrow.

I drink the last of my beer. I drive home.

PETE BURGER

When I wake it is dark, but I hear voices and the sounds of an engine and traffic. We're moving, and I have the worst hangover of my life.

"How much'd he say?" a woman says.

"Fifty big ones," Hi-Lo says.

"We're splitting it, right?" another woman says.

"Four ways, after expenses," Hi-Lo says.

I try to move, but my legs and arms won't respond, like they don't belong to me.

"Wait a second, what expenses?" I recognize Jasmine's voice. Her accent is gone.

"Whad'you think you used to paralyze him, Nyquil?" Ponytail says. "That stuff's expensive."

"Yeah, plus the travel and such," Hi-Lo says.

A rag is stuffed into my mouth and tied securely in place. I cry out, but whatever sound I make is smothered by the rag.

"Guys, sounds like he's awake," Maylin says in perfect English.

She opens the trunk lid. I am in the back of a van. Headlights shine in through the rear windows and illuminate Maylin's face.

"Hey there," she says. "Sorry we had to pack you up like that. It won't be long."

"Why are you talking to him?" Ponytail says.

"Just being nice."

"Leave him the fuck alone," Hi-Lo says.

"Hey there," Maylin says, putting her finger on my face. I can barely feel it. "Can't we get him out of there?"

"No," Hi-Lo says. "He stays in the trunk. We're almost there. Close the lid and leave him alone."

"What are they going to do with him?" Jasmine says.

"They're going to cut him up and film it," Ponytail says.

"No fucking way," Jasmine says.

"Market's huge. People pay thousands per copy. They get off on the stuff."

"But it's all fake, right?" Jasmine says. "It's not like they really cut him up or anything."

"Yeah, sure."

"They use a chainsaw," Hi-Lo says. "You want the maximum footage you can get from every subject. You don't want them bleeding to death right away."

An unrelenting coldness begins in my stomach.

"Nobody ever told me nothing about that," Jasmine says.

"Whad'you think we were going to do with this geek, adopt him?" Ponytail says.

"The arrangement I made," Hi-Lo says, "was to deliver one male, preferably under thirty years, of any race, height, or weight, with all his parts and appendages. They were very clear about that. They said he couldn't be missing anything."

"I don't know about this," Jasmine says.

"Yes, you do know," Ponytail says. "Bitch, you knew it all along. Nobody's ever paid you this kind of money for a little sex. You knew what this shit was all about."

"Don't fuckin' disrespect me."

"Why don't you two just shut the fuck up?" Hi-Lo says. "It's too late for this shit. And there's no way I'm letting either of you fuck this up now."

"Just do the math," Ponytail says. "That's all I'm saying. OK? Do the math, and you won't feel so bad."

"He's right. All that money for a few hours of work," Hi-Lo says.

"And there's more of them where that one came from," Ponytail says.

The coldness inflates and expands in all directions, into my chest and down my legs and arms, until it overtakes my hands and fingers.

"People," Maylin says, "can you please shut up? You're scaring him."

"Hey," Hi-Lo says. "Didn't you hear what I said?"

Maylin looks at me and smiles. I want to think that she is sorry for all this, that it's just a joke that got out of hand, that everything will be all right. I want to see that in her smile, in her eyes. I try to say something, to cry out, but there is no sound. "I wonder what it feels like," she says, looking at me.

My eyes fill with tears and she goes out of focus.

"I told you to shut the lid!" Hi-Lo yells.

The tears roll down the sides of my face and I can see her again.

Using both hands, Maylin lifts her top and shows me her breasts, moving her chest both ways so I can get a good look. Behind us, a car horn blows in short bursts. Her skin is very white in the flashing high beams.

"Shut the fuckin' lid!" Hi-Lo's screaming.

She pulls her top back in place before she goes out of focus once more.

"Now!"

The lid drops shut.

Acknowledgments

Thanks to the LZ Francis Foundation for endowing the Bakeless prizes. Special thanks to Francine Prose, Brandy Vickers, Jayne Yaffe Kemp, and Janet Silver. By welcoming me to the republic of letters, they have given me more than they will ever know.

Bread Loaf and the Bakeless Prizes

The Katharine Bakeless Nason Literary Publication Prizes were established in 1995 to expand Bread Loaf Writers' Conference's commitment to the support of emerging writers. Endowed by the LZ Francis Foundation, the prizes commemorate Middlebury College patron Katharine Bakeless Nason and launch the publication career of a poet, fiction writer, and creative nonfiction writer annually. Winning manuscripts are chosen in an open national competition by a distinguished judge in each genre. Winners are published by Houghton Mifflin Company in Mariner paperback original.

2005 Judges
Philip Levine, poetry
Francine Prose, fiction
Edward Hoagland, creative nonfiction

LaVergne, TN USA
06 February 2011
215414LV00007B/61/P